D0208210

The Twelve Dates of Christmas

How NOT to Spend Your Senior Year
BY CAMERON DOKEY

Royally Jacked
BY NIKI BURNHAM

Ripped at the Seams
BY NANCY KRULIK

Spin Control
BY NIKI BURNHAM

Cupidity
BY CAROLINE GOODE

South Beach Sizzle
BY SUZANNE WEYN AND DIANA GONZALEZ

She's Got the Beat
BY NANCY KRULIK

30 Guys in 30 Days
BY MICOL OSTOW

Animal Attraction
BY JAMIE PONTI

A Novel Idea
BY AIMEE FRIEDMAN

Scary Beautiful
BY NIKI BURNHAM

Getting to Third Date
BY KELLY McCLYMER

Dancing Queen
BY ERIN DOWNING

Major Crush
BY JENNIFER ECHOLS

Do-Over
BY NIKI BURNHAM

Love Undercover
BY JO EDWARDS

Prom Crashers
BY ERIN DOWNING

Gettin' Lucky
BY MICOL OSTOW

The Boys Next Door
BY JENNIFER ECHOLS

In the Stars
BY STACIA DEUTSCH AND RHODY COHON

Crush du Jour
BY MICOL OSTOW

The Secret Life of a Teenage Siren
BY WENDY TOLIVER

Love, Hollywood Style
BY P.J. RUDITIS

Something Borrowed
BY CATHERINE HAPKA

Party Games
BY WHITNEY LYLES

Puppy Love
BY NANCY KRULIK

Available from Simon Pulse

the romantic comedies

The Twelve Dates of Christmas

CATHERINE HAPKA

Simon Pulse
New York London Toronto Sydney

If you purchased this book without a cover, you should be aware that this book is stolen property. It was reported as "unsold and destroyed" to the publisher, and neither the author nor the publisher has received any payment for this "stripped book."

This book is a work of fiction. Any references to historical events, real people, or real locales are used fictitiously. Other names, characters, places, and incidents are the product of the author's imagination, and any resemblance to actual events or locales or persons, living or dead, is entirely coincidental.

SIMON PULSE
An imprint of Simon & Schuster Children's Publishing Division
1230 Avenue of the Americas, New York, NY 10020
Copyright © 2008 by Catherine Hapka
All rights reserved, including the right of reproduction in whole or in part in any form.
SIMON PULSE and colophon are registered trademarks of Simon & Schuster, Inc.
Designed by Ann Zeak
The text of this book was set in Garamond 3.
Manufactured in the United States of America
First Simon Pulse edition October 2008
10 9 8 7 6 5 4 3 2 1
Library of Congress Control Number 2008924797
ISBN-13: 978-1-4169-6412-4
ISBN-10: 1-4169-6412-6

The Twelve Dates of Christmas

Prologue

It had seemed like the perfect plan—get my boyfriend to fall for another girl, and I'd be free. No muss, no fuss, no guilt or bad feelings.

I'd approached it logically, like the scientific person I am. I'd identified the problem. I'd come up with a hypothesis. I'd set up an experiment.

And now the results were sitting across the warm, garlic-scented, holiday-bedecked room from me. Or, rather, getting up and walking out of said room, namely Manfredi's, my hometown's fanciest restaurant.

Cam glanced over toward me as he was helping his new girlfriend, Jaylene, with her coat. He smiled and waved. I returned the smile weakly and wriggled my fingers in return.

"What are you looking at, Lexi?" My date, Andrew Cole, stopped talking about himself just long enough to notice I wasn't hanging on his every word. He looked over at the door just in time to see the happy couple depart. "Oh." He shrugged, then shoveled in a mouthful of lasagna before returning to his favorite topic. "So anyway, like I was saying, the admissions guy from Northwestern told me that if I applied, he was positive I'd get in, and . . ."

I picked up my fork and poked at my pasta. But my stomach recoiled at the thought of actually eating it. I'd lost my appetite the second I'd walked into the restaurant and spotted Cam and Jaylene together.

Andrew had, in his efficient, over-achiever way, procured us a great table by the front window. It was tinted with fake frost and draped with garlands of holly and ivy, but that wasn't enough to block my view of Cam and Jaylene as they emerged onto the sidewalk outside. I watched them out of the corner of my eye, not wanting to see any more but unable to resist. Call it scientific curiosity.

It was early December and the temperature out there was normal for late evening in our part of Wisconsin—in other words, frigid. A few snowflakes drifted lazily down, lending the perfect touch to the scene. Seeing that we were in Claus Lake, that scene could be summed up in one word: Christmassy. The whole town was crazy for Christmas. Red and green lights twinkled up and down the poles of the streetlights, across the facades of all the shops on Elf Street, and even on the parking meters and stop signs. Holly and mistletoe were everywhere.

Jaylene huddled in her baby blue, fake-fur-trimmed, not-really-warm-enough-for-Wisconsin jacket, laughing at something Cam had just said. Then she let out an elaborate shiver and cocked her little blond hatless head up to say something to Cam, who was almost a foot taller than her. I couldn't hear them through the window, but I imagined her saying something like, *We-all don' have this heah wh-aht stuff fallin' outta the skah awl the tah-yam back home in Jaw-ja.*

Okay, so maybe her Southern accent isn't quite *that* bad. But it's close.

Anyway, whatever she said made Cam laugh. Now, a lot of people can laugh wickedly or sarcastically or wearily or even just politely. But not Cam. His whole face always lit up with pure joy whenever he smiled or laughed, like a little boy's on—well, okay, Christmas.

So he laughed, and then he put his arm around her. She snuggled up against him with another shiver, wrapping both her white-mittened hands around his waist.

She smiled up at him. He smiled down at her. A second later she was standing on tiptoes, and he was bending down toward her.

Their kiss sent an electric shock through me. A spontaneous kiss on a snowy evening, not knowing or caring who might see—since when had Cam become such a romantic?

And more important, since when did I *care*? After all, this was all totally my idea, my plan, my fault.

But maybe I need to backtrack a little. Begin at the beginning. See, it all really started a few months ago at the big last-day-of-freedom party at the lake the night before my first day of senior year. . . .

One

"Hold still."

I froze on command. A second later my best friend, Allie Lin, smacked me soundly on the forehead. "Ow!" I yelped.

"Mosquito," she explained succinctly.

I rubbed the spot. "Oh. Thanks."

She slapped herself on the arm, then shifted positions on the big old scratchy pine log where we were sitting. Her gaze drifted to a group of beefy-looking guys in Bermuda shorts over near the bonfire. They were pounding beers and talking football. Their loud, excited voices blended with the hip-hop music pouring out of the speakers of the battered old Chevy sedan parked on the rocky lakeside beach. The dark, still water of Lake Claus lapped gently against the car's front tires.

"I can't believe school starts tomorrow and I still don't have a boyfriend." Allie glanced from the football guys over to a couple making out furiously on the next log. "If I don't have a guy of my own before the Ball, I swear I'm going to give it up and become a nun."

In Claus Lake, there was only one thing people meant when they said "the Ball." That was the town's big Christmas Eve Costume Ball, held every year at the fireman's hall. It was a fund-raiser for some local charities, but more important, it was the social event of the season. The Christmas season, that is. And in Claus Lake, the Christmas season was the only season that counted. It lasted for a good four months, and people talked about it all year long.

"You can't become a nun," I reminded Allie. "You're not Catholic."

"Thanks, Logic Girl." She made a face at me. "My point is, I really, really, *really* don't want to go to the Ball stag this year."

I didn't see the big deal. The Ball wasn't a big date-night thing like homecoming or the prom. Lots of people went as couples, but plenty more went on their own or with their whole families or a bunch of friends or whatever. It wasn't important who you went with; it was just important that you *went*.

But I knew Allie didn't want to hear it. For the past three years, she'd gone to the Ball with me; my boyfriend, Cameron Kehoe; and my cousin Nicholas. However, last year Nick's girlfriend, Rachel, had been part of the gang too, suddenly making it feel much less like a group thing and more like a double date plus one. I guess Allie hadn't liked the feeling, because she seemed determined not to let it happen again this year.

"Senior year," she mused. "It hardly seems possible, does it? It seems like two seconds ago that we were all scared, stupid freshmen."

"What hardly seems possible is that I'll ever get everything done this fall." I stretched out my long legs, accidentally kicking over an abandoned beer bottle with one flip-flopped foot. "I need to finish up my college applications, sign up for the SATs, interview for the Simpson Scholarship—"

"It's not like you have to worry about

that last part," Allie interrupted, slapping another mosquito on her neck. "You have the Simpson Scholarship in the bag."

"Don't be so sure. Andrew Cole could weasel in there and get it instead of me, especially if I screw up the interview."

I frowned slightly at the thought. Every year, the Simpson Scholarship went to Claus Lake High School's most accomplished senior. Just having the highest GPA—which I did—was no guarantee. The committee was headed by Mrs. Alice Simpson, the town's wealthiest citizen, as well as one of its oldest at ninety-three and counting. Grades and academic achievements were very important, but so were extracurriculars, charity work, and who knew what else. Then there was the personal interview. That could make or break you with the committee—especially Mrs. Simpson.

Andrew had had the second-highest GPA in our class for the past three years running. He was also kind of charming in a geeky-nerdy, Clark Kent-y, sucking-up-to-adults kind of way. If he ended up winning that scholarship, I would probably have to reconsider my choice of colleges. And that would definitely be a total disaster.

See, I had my whole life pretty much planned out. My one-year plan was to win the Simpson Scholarship and get into a top East Coast university. Five-year plan: Earn a degree in biology and acceptance to the med school of my choice. Ten-plus-year plan: Begin fabulous career in medical research, complete with exciting big-city lifestyle.

I could hardly wait. But for now here I was, sitting with my best friend, listening to a good song, on a nice—albeit rather buggy and muggy—early September night. Not such a bad place to be, really. At least for the moment.

Reaching back over my head, I grabbed two fistfuls of my thick, springy auburn hair, lifting it up off the nape of my neck to take advantage of the slight breeze coming in off the lake. Even though the sun had set, it was hot and sticky. Sitting so close to the fire wasn't helping matters. If I hadn't known it was biologically impossible, I might have suspected I could melt into a puddle at any moment.

If the heat was affecting Allie the same way, she wasn't showing it. Her glossy dark chin-length hair was pulled back into a tiny ponytail at the back of her head, and her heart-shaped face was sweat free. As a new song came on the car radio she started bouncing and wriggling on the log, tapping her toes and shaking her slim shoulders in time to the music.

"Sit still, will you?" I complained. "You're making me sweat just watching you."

"Can't," she said, a little breathless from all the seat dancing. "Halfway There Theory, remember?"

That's another thing about Allie. She was always coming up with all these psychological theories, mostly about love and romance. She planned to write self-help books someday—you know, the kind with titles like *Visualize Your Way to a Hot, Happening Love Life* or *It's Not You, It's Him.* It was pretty much her life goal to get on *Oprah* with one of her bestselling tomes.

And now that she mentioned it, I did remember this particular theory. It was one of her favorites, one she'd trotted out on numerous occasions. It posited that if a girl wriggled and toe-tapped as if she were dancing right there in her seat, a guy would be more likely to come over and ask her to dance.

"Oh, right," I joked. "The Crazy Legs Theory. How could I forget? Isn't that the one we disproved at the prom? And then at Mary Zimmer's party? And then again at your aunt's wedding last month?"

"It only has to work once." Allie smiled serenely as she boogied down on the log.

I grinned. I was always amused by Allie's endless parade of new theories. That didn't mean I actually *believed* most of them—I was too much of a hard-science girl for that sort of thing—but luckily Allie was a good sport and didn't seem to mind that I often couldn't resist applying the scientific method to her so-called data.

The bonfire was dying down by now, and the crowd was starting to thin out. The football guys wandered down to the water's edge to throw rocks or something. Meanwhile couples had been slipping off into the darkness together for a while. Last chance for some carefree romance before the daily grind started up again.

That reminded me: I hadn't seen Cam in quite some time. However, it only took a quick glance around to locate him. He was over on the far side of the fire, picking up empty cans and bottles and tossing them into the public recycling bin near the fire pit.

Yeah. Way romantic. Then again, that was kind of the way things had been going with us lately.

I guess Allie heard my sigh and followed my gaze toward Cam. "What's wrong?" she demanded. "You're not still worried that you and Cam are losing your spark, are you?"

"Maybe a little," I admitted.

It was true. The closer we got to senior year, the more I thought about what came next—after high school. And the more I looked forward to my carefully planned out, totally fabu future, the more I realized there was one thing I hadn't taken into account while making those plans. Namely, my almost-four-year relationship with Cam.

Don't get me wrong. Cam was a great guy. Everybody said so, from Allie and Nick to my parents to the little old ladies whose groceries Cam helped bring in every weekend. Yeah, he was that nice.

And maybe that was part of the problem. I wasn't one to psychoanalyze myself or anything, but I couldn't help wondering if there was something missing between me and Cam. I guess those thoughts might have started when Nick got together with Rachel. From the beginning the two of them couldn't keep their hands off each other. They were always hugging or kissing or just walking along all intertwined. Once I noticed that, I started noticing that a lot of other couples were the same way. Touchy-feely. Staring into each other's eyes. That sort of thing.

Cam and I weren't like that. I wasn't sure we'd ever been like that. Did that mean we were missing something? Or had our relationship run its course? Had we grown apart without really noticing? Were we just stuck now in a state of stasis? My scientific mind was pretty sure it had a strong hypothesis about that, and it was getting harder to ignore the evidence.

Allie was staring at me. She'd even forgotten to keep up her seat dancing.

"You realize you're nuts, right?" she said. "Cam is *such* an amazing guy. One of a kind. And you two are perfect together." She shook her head so vigorously that a strand of hair came loose from her tiny ponytail. "All this crazy talk about breaking up is probably just fear of success or something." Her eyes lit up. "Hey, I like that! I could call it the Scared to Splitsville Theory."

I rolled my eyes. "Please," I said. "Since when do I have a fear of success? I *love* success. I embrace it. I seek it out and coddle it and call it pet names."

"I'm not talking about school and stuff." The song on the car radio changed, and Allie suddenly seemed to remember her dancing. She started bouncing in time to the beat again while she talked. "Everybody has some kind of fear of success. Maybe yours has to do with love. Like, you didn't choose Cam through some scientific theorem, so you're not convinced that your relationship should work as well as it does, and now you're trying to sabotage it to prove yourself right. Ooh!" She looked even more excited; she always gets that way when she thinks she's figured someone out. Usually me. "That totally makes sense. You're used to always being right—you know, with the good grades and stuff—and so this has been eating you up inside and made you *want* to be wrong this time."

Before I could point out all the flaws in that reasoning, Bruce Janssen came loping over to us. Bruce was one of Cam's best guy friends, though I wasn't sure why, since he was pretty much Cam's opposite in every way. He was the type of guy who thinks other people are truly impressed that he can fart the first two bars of "The Star-Spangled Banner." He was probably planning to put that on his college applications.

He skidded to a stop in front of us. "Hey, Michaels," he greeted me.

I automatically drew in my legs as his pale-green eyes slid down them. Bracing myself, I waited for his sleazy compliment of the day. What would it be this time? Maybe how he'd dreamed about my legs last night. Or how just once before he died he wanted to know how it felt to bury his hands in my wild, luxurious hair. Even Cam had rolled his eyes the first time Bruce came out with that one. Then again, maybe he'd just call me "Sexy Lexi" and try to grope me—after all, everyone loves a classic.

However, this time Bruce turned toward Allie. "Lookin' good, Lin," he said, tossing his too-long blond hair out of his eyes. "Wanna dance?"

"Sure!" Allie bounced out of her seat.

I hid a smile. It was obvious that Allie

was so excited that her Crazy Legs Theory had finally worked, she'd forgotten all about another of her favorite theories: the Never Dance with Losers Theory.

I watched as she and Bruce made their way over to a smooth spot on the beach where a few other couples were dancing. Allie immediately went from slapping mosquitoes to slapping Bruce's hands away from everywhere they weren't supposed to be.

Just then I saw Cam coming toward me. I guess he'd finally noticed the romantic mood. Or maybe he'd just seen me sitting alone and his Mr. Nice Guy side had kicked in automatically.

"Hey," he said, sitting down on the log beside me.

"Hey back," I replied, taking in that familiar sweet, handsome, square-jawed face, and his kind eyes and broad shoulders. Maybe Allie was right. Maybe I was silly to question being with a guy like that. I put my hand on his knee and squeezed, figuring a little romantic moment of our own might help chase the anxious thoughts away. "Having a nice time tonight?"

"Sure." Cam smiled, but he looked kind

of distracted. He glanced around. "Hey, did you meet that guy Mike from Dornerville? Tall guy in the red T-shirt? I was talking to him a few minutes ago, and it turns out his mom works at the financial aid office at the campus over there. He thinks she can put in a word for me. Nice of him, huh?"

That brought me back to earth with a thud. Cam wasn't really the ambitious type. He seemed perfectly content to attend the nearest state university satellite campus to study culinary arts and business. He expected to use that education to get a job as an assistant chef somewhere, with the idea of someday opening his own restaurant right there in Claus Lake. We didn't talk about it much, but I hadn't been able to miss the fact that those plans didn't mesh too well with my own big-career, big-city dreams.

Cam finally seemed to notice my hand on his knee. He covered it with his own hand, rubbing my palm with his thumb.

"But listen," he said softly, wrapping his free arm around me and pulling me closer, "why worry about school on our last night of freedom, right?"

I did my best to push aside my worries

once again. The future wasn't here yet. Maybe I could wait one more night to worry about it.

"Uh-huh." I turned and swung my legs over his lap, then leaned closer. My shoulder fit into the crook of his arm in its usual familiar way, and I could smell mint on his breath as his lips found mine.

The sound of squealing tires interrupted our kiss. I pulled back and glanced over Cam's shoulder toward the parking lot.

"Hey," I said in surprise, recognizing the car that had just peeled in and screeched to a zigzaggy stop across a couple of empty spaces. "Looks like Nick came after all."

That was unexpected. My cousin's girlfriend was a year older than the rest of us, and she was leaving for the University of Michigan the next day. Nick had spent the whole past week planning a big, romantic night that was supposed to tide them over until the first weekend visit.

But now here he was, climbing out of his car with his sandy hair standing on end and his polo shirt askew. Even in the dim light of the crescent moon and the fading bonfire, I could tell from his face that something was wrong.

Cam had turned to look by now too. "Whoa, he looks upset." Gently shoving me off his lap, he stood up and hurried toward Nick.

I was right behind him. When we reached Nick, I could see he was even worse off than I'd thought. He was practically hyperventilating—very un-Nick-like. Normally Nick is the type of guy who would smile in front of a firing squad and ask for a cigarette. And he doesn't even smoke. I'd known him since birth—we'd grown up next door to each other, more like sister and brother than cousins—and I'd never seen him lose his cool like this.

"Lex," he choked out. "Cam."

"What is it?" I grabbed his arm, resisting the urge to shake him. "Is someone hurt? Is it Mom or Dad? Or *your* mom or dad? What? *Who?*"

Nick waved his hand around vaguely. "No. No. Nothing like that. Everyone's fine."

"Then what?" I demanded.

"Lexi . . . ," Cam murmured soothingly.

Nick shook his head. "No," he croaked. "It's just . . . just . . . just Rachel."

Cam and I traded a confused look. "What do you mean, buddy?" Cam asked gently. "What about Rachel? Is she okay?"

Nick squeezed his eyes shut for a second, then opened them and stared at us bleakly. "She dumped me," he said hoarsely. "Just now. Said she—um, she didn't want to see me tied down when she was off, you know, living her new life in college."

Cam probably said all the right things after that—he usually does—but I was so shocked that I couldn't react at first. Nick and Rachel had seemed like the perfect couple from day one. I'd thought those two would be together forever. *Everyone* had thought that. Well, everyone but Rachel, apparently.

So what did "together forever" really mean, anyway?

Two

"Actuate," Allie said. "Definition, please. I'll give you a hint—it's a verb."

I took a sip of my strawberry milk shake, then drummed my fingers on the paper place mat in front of me. "Actuate," I said. "To move or incite into action."

"Very good. Now use it in a sentence."

I glanced around the crowded Elf Street Diner for inspiration. "Um, I need to actuate myself into deciding what to do about me and Cam."

Allie had just popped a french fry into her mouth. She frowned, then quickly chewed and swallowed. "Very funny," she said. "You're not still thinking about that, are you? I figured that was just end-of-summer doldrums or something."

It had been a little over a week since the bonfire, and Allie and I had been way too busy since then to sit around discussing my relationship. School had started, and the teachers seemed determined to head off any early bouts of Senioritis by assigning boatloads of homework. On top of that, my mom and aunt were both on the committee for the Christmas Eve Costume Ball again this year, which meant that Nick and I, plus all our friends, were automatically drafted into service as well. Joy to the world.

"I don't know," I told Allie with a sigh. "I keep trying to look at it logically, you know?"

Allie shoved away her list of SAT vocabulary words, almost pushing it into the water ring her soda glass had left behind on the table. "Okay," she said. "If you want to get all science-nerdy about this and do the whole pro-con thing, think about it this way. Isn't it nice not having to worry about who you're going with to the homecoming dance? Or the Ball? Or the prom?"

"No argument there," I admitted. "It's

definitely easier not having to worry about those things. Especially since Cam is still always fun to hang out with. No complaints there." I shrugged and played with my straw. "But is that enough reason to stay with someone? Is it fair to either of us?"

"Of course it is!" Allie exclaimed. "You guys care about each other. That's all that matters. Love conquers all, right?"

"Does it?" I leaned forward, gazing at her across the table. "Seriously, Allie, think about it. After this year, I'll be off to college at least, like, eight hundred miles away. Meanwhile Cam is probably going to wind up staying right here in Wisconsin."

"So what?" Allie's lower lip jutted out stubbornly. "Lots of people have made that kind of thing work."

I shrugged. "Okay, granted. But trying to keep up a long-distance relationship through four years of college is bad enough. What happens after that? Our goals and visions of life are just so different."

"Right, and that's what I've always said makes you guys so perfect together," Allie said. "Opposites Attract Theory, remember?"

Fine. If she was going to start throwing

her theories in my face, two could play that game.

"Okay, then what about the Testing the Waters Theory?" I asked her. "You know, the one you came up with a while back that says nobody should just glom on to the first guy or girl who ever asks them out on a date. Neither Cam nor I have ever had any other serious relationships. How do we know the grass isn't greener somewhere else?"

"Oh, please." Allie rolled her eyes. "That theory doesn't apply to you guys."

"Why not? Besides, most relationships end at some point, especially for people our age. I'm sure there's plenty of statistical evidence about that. Why should I expect to be the exception?"

She frowned. "Why do you have to be so logical about everything?" she said. "Anyway, if you want to break up with Cam, just do it already. I can't stop you." She stuffed another fry in her mouth, then mumbled, "Even if I do know for a fact that it would be the hugest mistake of your life."

I didn't bother to argue with her usage of the term *fact*. I already knew that would be pointless.

"It's not that I *want* to break up with him," I said instead. "I just think it's probably inevitable, that's all. Sad, but necessary." With that, I decided to back off. It was obvious that Allie was getting kind of upset. She could be pretty sensitive about that sort of thing. "Anyway, give me another word, okay? The Simpson Scholarship won't help much if I blow the verbal on the SAT."

That much was logical enough not to allow any argument. I knew I could ace the math part of the test even sound asleep and with one hand tied behind my back. However, I was a lot weaker on vocabulary. Luckily Allie is a word whiz. Must be from reading all those self-help books she loves so much. They probably have to get pretty creative to keep coming up with new ways to tell women how to land their dream guys.

"Fine." Allie pulled the vocab list toward her again and scanned it. "Here are a few words for you. I offer you my sincerest adjuration to abrogate this abstruse and abhorrent aberration. Quit being so contumacious about it, or I shall have to berate you."

I was still puzzling through that one when the jingle bells hanging on the door started jangling. Glancing that way, I saw Nick dragging himself into the diner. His face wore the hangdog, depressed look that had become all too familiar over the past week.

"Nick!" Allie waved at him. "Over here."

He blinked and then shambled over. "Hey," he said. "What's up?"

"I'm just trying to talk Lexi out of doing something really stupid," Allie informed him.

Nick flopped into the booth beside me. "So what else is new?" he said with a shadow of his old humor.

"Don't listen to her." I shot Allie a warning look. Now didn't seem to be the time to involve Nick in a debate about me and Cam. He was depressed enough already. "We're just running some vocabulary words. Want to join in?"

"Sure." He shrugged. "Might take my mind off—well, you know."

"That's true," Allie said. "I have a theory about that, actually; I'm calling it the Broody Brain Theory. The idea is that if you're filling your mind with new knowledge, you won't have any brain cells left for moping over your love life or whatever."

I laughed. Normally Nick would've joined in. He loves making fun of Allie's theories almost as much as I do.

But not today. He just sighed deeply and picked at the edge of the table. "It'll take more than a few vocabulary words to take my mind off Rachel," he mumbled.

I winced. *Pathetic* used to be the last word anyone would ever use to describe Nick. But these days, sadly, it fit him perfectly. I wished there was something I could do to help him snap out of it, but so far he only seemed interested in wallowing.

That brought my mind back to Cam again. It had been bad enough thinking about breaking things off with him before. I hadn't been sure I'd have the heart—or the guts—to actually ever go through with it. If I did, I knew it would take some real finesse. Even if we weren't meant to be a couple, I knew for certain that I always wanted us to be friends. Besides, I didn't want to mess up our tight little group—Allie and Nick would never forgive me if I did. I'd never forgive myself.

But now, watching Nick brood over his ex, the idea of breaking up with Cam seemed even harder to imagine. Nick was really devastated; who knew how long it would take him to get over Rachel? And he wasn't anywhere near as sweet and sensitive as Cam. How could I possibly put Cam through that kind of heartbreak? How would I ever be able to stand watching him go through that?

"Lexi, are you even listening to me?" Allie's annoyed voice broke into my thoughts. "Because I really didn't think that *ruminate* was that hard a word."

"Sorry. Um, *ruminate* means to think something over."

"Right," Allie said.

Nick glanced over at me. "Way to ruminate your way through that one, science geekette," he said, once again sounding almost like his old self for a second. "Maybe you'll be able to get that verbal score within two hundred points of the math one after all."

I laughed, doing my best to push all ruminations about Cam out of my head, at least for the moment. What was the hurry, anyway? This wasn't a bio lab with a time limit. Just because I'd identified a possible problem didn't mean I had to rush out and solve it right away.

✯

One afternoon a couple of weeks later, Cam came over to help me prep for my Simpson Scholarship interview, which was scheduled for the following day. I have to admit, I was a little tense about it. Verging on hysterical.

"What if I screw this up?" I asked him for about the tenth time, pacing back and forth across my living room. "What if I don't get the scholarship?"

He was splayed out on the big squishy beige couch. My parents were both out, so we had the place to ourselves aside from Blitzen, the family cat, who was sleeping on the couch beside Cam. Sitting up carefully to avoid jostling the cat—she could be cranky when awakened suddenly—Cam gave me that easy smile that always made me feel a little calmer.

"Chill out, Lexi," he said. "You're going to do great tomorrow. Mrs. Simpson will love you."

"But what if she doesn't?" I argued, still pacing. "I might, you know, forget myself and accidentally blurt out the F-word or something."

He laughed out loud at that. "Right,"

he said with a twinkle in his eye. "I'm sure that's really likely to happen."

"Okay, maybe not." I sighed and ran both hands through my hair, even though I knew that always made me end up looking like Bozo the Clown. "This is just so important, you know?"

"I know."

I stopped pacing and stared down at him. "Do you?" I asked. "I mean, you never really seem to think about the future much. Where do you see yourself in five years?"

"We've talked about this before, Lexi." He reached for my hand and pulled me down until I was sitting beside him. Blitzen woke up and shot me a baleful look before slinking off. "I'll get my degree, then probably look for a job where I can learn the restaurant business from the bottom up. Maybe open a little place of my own someday."

"Okay," I said slowly, "but have you ever noticed that your goals and mine—well, they don't exactly match?"

"I guess." He didn't sound terribly concerned. "But why worry about that before we have to? The future will take care of itself. We just need to try to be happy now and figure out the rest when it comes."

I gritted my teeth. "Are you kidding?" I cried. "That sounds like one of Allie's crazy theories or something. What if the future *doesn't* work itself out? What then?"

He just shrugged. "I don't know. It always does, though."

Almost everything about Cam was great. But that default attitude of his—*oh well, it'll work itself out*—always made me crazy, even when he was just talking about finding a parking spot or something. But this time it was much worse. This time he was talking about our whole future. *My* whole future. How could he be so infuriatingly casual about it?

"Did I ever tell you how I decided to go into medical research?" I asked, determined to make him understand for once just how important this was.

"Sure." He shifted in his seat, slinging one arm across the couch behind me. "It was when your mom got sick when you were a kid, right?"

"That was part of it." I nodded. "When I was six or seven Mom had a cancer scare, and our whole family traveled to the Mayo Clinic to have it checked out."

"Yeah, I remember now." Cam reached

down and squeezed my upper arm. "That must have been really scary for you."

"Uh-huh, I guess." I stared blankly at the mirror over the fireplace across the room, barely feeling his hand as I thought back to that time. Back then I hadn't even really understood exactly what cancer was. I'd just known it was something bad. "Anyway, it turned out to be a false alarm, thank God. Everything was benign; Mom was fine. But while we were at the clinic and she was getting her tests done and stuff, there was this one doctor who was supernice to me. He kept an eye on me while Dad was distracted, and even took me on a tour of his lab and let me play with his ultrasound machine."

"Nice of him," Cam said.

I nodded. "I'm sure he was busy. All those docs always are. But he took the time to watch out for me, and I always remembered that, even though I don't even know his name. Ever since then I've known I wanted to do what he did. I asked Mom and Dad recently if they remembered who he was so I could mention him in my college application essays, but they don't remember either. So I just wrote the essays without the name."

"That's a great story," Cam said. "I bet the college admissions people will love it."

"I hope so. But that's not my point. I know we all kid around about how driven I am, how I plan out everything in my life and stuff. I guess I'm trying to tell you just how much those plans mean to me."

He reached over and gently pushed a lock of auburn hair out of my face, smiling down at me fondly. "I get that," he said, his fingers tracing the outline of my forehead. "I always have, Lexi. It's part of what makes you, you."

His expression was so caring and happy that I didn't have the heart to go on. I did my best to tamp down my own frustration, but it wasn't easy. If he really *did* understand, wouldn't he be a little more worried that our futures were so completely mismatched?

Three

"So when do you find out about the scholarship?" Nick asked, carefully threading a cranberry onto a piece of fishing line.

"Weren't you listening? She already said she doesn't know." Allie grabbed a pair of scissors from the floor and snipped off the end of the cranberry garland she'd just finished. "But it doesn't matter, anyway. It sounds like she totally blew them away at the interview. That scholarship is so hers."

"Don't jinx me," I warned her. "Yeah, I think I did pretty well in that interview. Still, Andrew might've done even better. You never know."

But my focus wasn't really on the Simpson Scholarship anymore. I'd done all

I could; from now on it was up to the committee, and I was trying not to stress over it too much. Besides, I had other things on my mind.

I grabbed another handful of cranberries. The three of us were sitting on the floor of Nick's roomy, yellow-walled basement rec room, stringing garlands. Nick's mom, my aunt, was head of decorations for the Ball that year, and even though it was still September, she already had us hard at work. There was a ton to do before December 24. At least she'd left us with plenty of soda and popcorn to help us through the day's task. Then again, maybe we were supposed to turn the popcorn into more garlands. If that was true, she was going to be sorely disappointed when she returned home from that day's round of committee meetings.

"Listen, guys," I said to my friends, grabbing another handful of popcorn out of the almost-empty bowl. "I want to talk to you about something. About Cam, actually."

Allie's head shot up, and she almost cut her own finger off with the scissors. "What?" she demanded. "You're not still actually thinking about ending things with Cam?"

"Sort of," I admitted. "I just keep going

back and forth on it, you know? It's driving me nuts. On the one hand, Cam is great."

"As I've been telling you all along," Allie put in with a frown.

"I know. And you're right." I shook my head. "But on the other hand, where are Cam and I headed, realistically speaking?"

"Homecoming," Allie put in. "The Ball. The prom."

"Right. But then what?"

Nick looked a little confused. He'd been so deep into his own heartache that I guess he wasn't fully up to speed on my love life issues. "Wait," he said. "You're not thinking of stringing Cam along until you're ready to leave for college and then ripping his heart out with your bare hands, are you?"

He sounded a little suspicious. And a lot bitter. Who could blame him?

"Definitely not," I assured him. "That's why I'm thinking about this now instead of putting it off. If Cam and I are going to end up going our separate ways next summer, why prolong the inevitable?"

"Because you guys are in love, that's why!" Allie exclaimed.

I barely heard her. All this time, I'd

been moving inexorably toward the only logical conclusion. No matter how many times I went over the facts, checked the variables, ran the numbers, the result was always the same.

"There's only one answer." I took a deep breath, ignoring the floppy-fish feeling in the pit of my stomach. That feeling was irrelevant to the facts. "Cam and I need to break up."

Allie gasped, her scissors clattering to the floor. Even Nick looked kind of shocked.

"Dude," he said. "Are you sure? Seriously, it'll kill him if you dump him out of the blue."

"Don't worry, I'm not planning to dump Cam at all." I smiled slowly as a great idea popped into my head. Who says scientists can't be creative? "No, I've just realized there's a much kinder, gentler way to handle this. I'm going to get *Cam* to break up with *me*!"

"Huh?" Allie looked perplexed. "What are you talking about, Lexi?"

"Yeah." Nick set down his threaded cranberries and peered at me suspiciously. "Since when do you play those kinds of games? You've always been a straight shooter."

I raised an eyebrow at him. "Actually, you were the inspiration for this plan."

"Me?" Nick blinked. "You're pinning this on *me*?"

"Yeah. Just look at you—Rachel dumped you almost a month ago, and you're still a mess. And you guys were together less than a year." I shook my head. "No way do I want to do that to Cam. It'll be way easier on him if I let him make the decision to end things."

"I hope you're not in a hurry," Allie said dubiously.

"I'm not," I replied, tossing a piece of popcorn into my mouth. "I won't rush it. These things take time."

"No." Allie shook her head. "I mean, I hope you aren't counting on Cam suddenly deciding to dump you anytime this century. Because it's not going to happen."

"She's right, Lex." Nick stretched out his legs and flicked a stray cranberry off the knee of his jeans. "The dude has it bad for you. He never even *looks* at other girls. Not even superhot, half-naked ones." He licked his lips. "Mmm, half-naked girls," he Homer Simpsoned.

I rolled my eyes. Maybe there was a

glimmer of light at the end of Nick's tunnel of heartbreak after all.

"Anyway," he went on, "if you're really set on ending things, you should just go ahead and do it. Cam is going to be totally devastated either way."

"Not if I do this right," I countered, the plan forming more fully in my mind even as I spoke. "All I have to do is set things up so he falls for another girl. That way, he'll realize for himself that we've been growing apart and then *he'll* break up with *me*." I shrugged. "He's too honest to do anything else once he's seen the light. And that way, no one's heart gets broken. If I handle it right, we can totally stay friends and enjoy the rest of senior year together without all the complications and wondering where our relationship is going and stuff. It's win-win. Totally foolproof!"

"You're nuts, Lexi," Allie said. "I'm telling you, it'll never work. Cam adores you."

"And I adore him." I sighed as they both stared at me with skepticism written all over their faces. Just because I was able to look at the situation logically, it didn't mean I didn't have feelings or that this wasn't tearing me up inside. "Listen, you guys, I wish I didn't have to do this. But I've been over all the options, and it's the only way. Cam and I are just too different. That's okay in high school, but we won't be in high school much longer. That means it's time for some tough choices. Like it or not."

Nick rolled his eyes. "Oh, please," he said, reaching for the popcorn bowl. "If you keep this up, you'll have to quit the Science Geekettes of America and join the drama club."

I reached over and gave him a shove. "I'm serious, smart guy," I said. "If you can think of a better idea to handle this, then spill it."

"I can think of a better idea," Allie put in. "Stay with Cam. Figure things out. Live happily ever after."

That was Allie for you. Hopeless romantic. "I already told you, that won't work," I said patiently. "How are we going to live happily ever after when I'm running a lab in Boston or New York or Atlanta and Cam's running a kitchen right here in Claus Lake?"

"But you guys are such a great couple!" Allie actually looked as if she might burst into tears. "I mean, okay, maybe you're not that much alike. But that's kind of what makes it work!"

"She's right, Lex," Nick agreed. "If you ever hooked up with someone as logical and ambitious as yourself, you'd drive each other crazy."

Yeah. He had a point. Then again, it wasn't really *the* point.

"Plus you guys have always been so happy together," Allie said. "You barely ever even fight or anything."

"I know we seem happy enough now," I said. "But we'll probably both be even happier once we've moved on. And it's not like we can't stay friends, like I said. In fact, I can't imagine not having Cam in my life one way or another."

That, as it turned out, was quite literally true. As I sat there, I tried to imagine it. Not having Cam around. Never talking to him, never hanging out together. Maybe never seeing him again after graduation.

But it didn't work. My mind couldn't seem to put together that kind of scenario. It just Did. Not. Compute.

I shrugged it off, deciding it didn't matter. If my plan worked out the way I was picturing it, there would be no need for me to imagine Life Without Cam. We could stay good friends, hang out for the rest of senior year and all next summer. Then when I went off to college, he'd still be there for me just like Allie and Nick, supporting me from a distance, giving me one of his patented pep talks as I dove off the high board of life into my exciting new future.

Meanwhile he would be free to figure out how to put his own future in motion. He could find himself a girl who would be perfectly content to stay in Claus Lake all her life, maybe hostessing at Cam's future restaurant and serving on the refreshments committee with him for the Ball. There were tons of girls at our school who would dream of nothing more, especially if the plan involved an amazing guy like Cam.

"I don't know, Lex." Nick still seemed dubious as he methodically scarfed down the rest of the popcorn. "Maybe you should think about this some more."

"Yeah," Allie agreed. "Don't forget about the Fast and Furious Theory. The quicker you try to make big moves or decisions in a relationship, the more likely it is to end in anger or heartache."

"You know, that theory actually *almost* makes sense," I said. "But it doesn't apply to me. Not unless almost four years counts as a quick move."

"You might as well give it up, Allie," Nick put in. "This is Lexi Michaels you're talking to, remember? Once her mind is made up, that's that. No turning back. Mule city."

I made a face at him. "Very funny," I said. "Why don't you just come out and call me stubborn?"

"I thought I just did." He shrugged. "But here you go, Ms. Literal. You're stubborn."

I laughed. Now that I'd finally made my decision, I was feeling a little better already. It was always kind of comforting to have a course of action, a plan to follow. No more looming uncertainties. Just a problem to be solved, sort of like an especially challenging and complex bio lab. Now that I had the gist of how to approach it, I just needed to nail down the details and I'd be all set.

"Okay, you guys." I leaned over to grab

the last few pieces of popcorn before Nick could polish them off. "So help me out here. It's time to set up a little social experiment. I need to get my boyfriend another woman!"

Four

Getting Cam a new girlfriend turned out to be a lot harder than I'd expected. In fact, for the first few weeks I wasn't sure I'd be able to pull it off after all.

For one thing, none of the girls at school seemed quite right for him. When I'd first concocted the plan, Claus Lake High School had seemed to be bursting with vaguely appropriate potential girlfriends for Cam. But once I got specific, it seemed every girl I considered had some fatal flaw. Carla Myers talked too much—if he ended up with her, poor Cam would never get a word in edgewise. Amalia Rozin was too quiet and passive. Cam wasn't the type of person who wanted to do *all* the talking and planning in a relationship. Patti Amundson was rumored to have cheated on her last boyfriend, and there was no way I was going to risk fixing Cam up with someone who might betray him. No, if this was going to work, I was going to have to find just the right girl. The perfect girl. The girl Cam deserved.

"What about Talia Lund?" Allie asked one day at lunch. She was still dragging her heels on this whole breaking-up-with-Cam thing. But at least she seemed to be trying to help.

I glanced across the school cafeteria at a pretty blond girl talking and laughing with her friends and shook my head. "You mean little miss peppy-peppy cheerleader?" I picked up my sandwich. "Ugh. I don't think so. Cam doesn't go for that type."

"Right." Allie rolled her eyes. "Funny how none of the girls we know seem to be good enough for Cam. Maybe this is the Maybe Not Theory in action? You know, you don't *really* want to go through with this, so you're sabotaging your own efforts?"

"Sorry, guess again." I paused to take a bite of my sandwich. "I'm just trying to be scientific about this," I added after I'd chewed and swallowed, "to give my plan the best chance to work. That means narrowing it down to the absolute best candidate before proceeding."

"Right." Allie pursed her lips and sort of smirked.

"Check it out," I said to Cam. "There's Margie Mendenhall. She looks really pretty in that outfit, doesn't she?"

He barely looked up from the pine garland he was attaching to a lamppost outside the fireman's hall. "Huh?" he said, glancing briefly at a girl walking her dog farther down the block. "Oh. I guess. But listen, that reminds me—we should start thinking about our costumes for the Ball soon. You know the good ones always go fast. What do you say we go as reindeer this year?"

"Maybe," I said. "But listen, did you know Margie's a really good cook? I heard she won some kind of recipe contest in some magazine last year. Maybe we should go ask her about it."

"Not right now, okay, sweetie?" Cam's tongue poked out of the corner of his mouth as he bent lower, totally focused on what he was doing. "Your aunt will kill us if we don't get these garlands up today."

Glancing down the street, I saw Margie round the corner and disappear. Maybe it was just as well Cam hadn't taken that particular bait. Sure, the two of them had that cooking interest in common. But while Margie was really sweet, I wasn't sure her sense of humor would mesh with Cam's that well.

I leaned back against a parking meter and shoved my hands in the pockets of my parka as I watched Cam finish hanging the garland. There was a definite nip in the air these days—October was almost half over, which meant the town's holiday preparations were in full swing. In Claus Lake, the arrival of October didn't mean it was time to put up the Halloween decorations, the way it probably did in most places. Nope, the only nod to All Hallow's Eve was maybe a witch's hat on the giant Santa outside the used car lot and some pumpkins mixed in with the mistletoe. It was pretty much Christmas-Christmas-Christmas from October 1 straight through the New Year.

Nick's mom being in charge of decorations for the Ball meant she was involved in decking more than just the hall. Before long there wouldn't be a square inch of Claus Lake that wasn't bedecked and holly jolly.

Helping out with that was keeping me pretty busy. So was my mom, who was cochair of the food committee and counting on me to help keep her organized and halfway sane. Then on top of that there were the SATs, my college applications, and of course the usual daily grind of schoolwork and so forth.

With all that going on in my life, was it any wonder my plan seemed to be stalled before it had begun?

One Sunday afternoon in late October, I answered the door expecting to find Mrs. Abernathy from next door, who was late for the food committee meeting currently taking place in the glassed-in sunroom at the back of the house. Instead I found Allie standing on the front porch, wrapped in her favorite down jacket and a long purple scarf.

"Come on in," I told her. "You're just in time to help me make coffee for Mom's committee. I can use the help, too. They're all caffeine fiends."

She grimaced, but came in anyway. "Listen, I can't stay long," she began, unwinding her scarf.

"Likely excuse," I joked. "Would it sweeten the deal if I told you there are cookies?"

She laughed. "No, I'm serious," she said. "Tommy gets home from soccer practice in, like, half an hour, and I told Mom I'd be there to meet him." Tommy was Allie's eleven-year-old brother. He was pretty much a computer freak. If someone wasn't there watching him, he'd spend all his time on the computer, to the exclusion of food, sleep, homework, and possibly breathing. "But first I really need to talk to you," Allie went on. "You know that girl Jaylene who lives across the street from me, right?"

"You mean the Southern belle of Willow Street?" Jaylene was a chatty, giggly bleached blond whose family had moved to town over the summer from somewhere south of Scarlett O'Haraville. "Yeah. What about her?"

"Well, you know she's still kind of new in town." Allie followed me into the kitchen, where the coffeepot was bubbling. The sounds of Mom and the rest of the committee chattering and laughing drifted faintly through the sliding glass doors in the breakfast nook. "So she doesn't know that many people yet."

"Really? She doesn't exactly seem like the shy type." Jaylene was a year behind us in school, but juniors and seniors shared the same lunch period. I'd noticed Allie's neighbor flirting with every guy in sight on numerous occasions. She was one of those people it was hard not to notice—and apparently the male population of Claus Lake High School agreed.

"Okay. But still, she's going to that fund-raising banquet for the new high school over in East Lake next weekend, and she asked me to help her find a date. She wants someone classy who looks good in a suit and tie." Allie shrugged. "So I thought of Nick. I've been worried about him—he's still really down about the whole Rachel thing. I thought maybe this would be a way to help him start moving on. But I wanted to check with you first to see if you think it's a good idea before I say anything to either Nick or Jaylene."

"Nick will never do it. He hates getting

dressed up and sitting around listening to speeches," I said automatically, though I wasn't really thinking about my cousin. I'd just had one of those flashes of inspiration that usually only hit me in the lab. "But I have a better idea—what about Cam?"

"What about him?" Allie looked genuinely confused for a second. Then her face cleared, and her eyes widened. "Wait, what? Are you serious?"

I shrugged. "Sure, why not? Cam will take her to that banquet if I ask him to. And who knows? Maybe spending the evening with another girl will be enough to finally jump-start my plan."

"Are you sure you're thinking of the right Jaylene?" Allie asked. "She doesn't really seem like his type. Besides, Cam hates sitting still for that long just as much as Nick does."

"I know, I know." I grabbed several coffee mugs out of the cabinet and lined them up on the counter. "Cam will be bored to death. And Jaylene is all wrong for him. But it doesn't matter. He hasn't picked up on any of my hints about more appropriate girls. So maybe the important thing is just to get him out there, spending time with someone else. Being on a date with a girl other than me. That way, he might get used to the idea and maybe want more. You know, kind of like Pavlov's dog."

"I don't know, Lexi." Allie sounded troubled. "This is Cam's life you're talking about here, not some science experiment. He's not going to suddenly decide he wants to date another girl—especially a girl like Jaylene—just because he's stuck with her for a few hours."

"You never know." I reached for the coffeepot and shot her a sly look. "What about that old Opposites Attract Theory you're always throwing in my face?"

She groaned and I chuckled, suddenly sure this was the right move. Okay, so Allie was right—there was no way Cam was going to suddenly fall for someone like Jaylene. She was giggly and prissy and high-maintenance and pushy and loud and maybe a teensy bit trashy, with her pink mohair sweaters, high heels with jeans, and baby blue eyeshadow. In other words, exactly the kind of girl Cam *didn't* like.

Still, I knew he would agree to the date

as long as I made it sound like he was doing Jaylene a big favor. He was like that. So what did I have to lose?

"A banquet?" Cam sounded dubious.

But I was prepared for that. "I know it's a drag," I said, reaching over to squeeze his hand. Not wanting to waste any time, I'd hurried over to his house as soon as I could get away from Mom's Merry Minions back at the committee meeting. "If you really don't want to do it, that's okay, but I promised Allie I'd ask. She's just worried that since Jaylene is new in town, she won't be able to find anyone to go with and might just decide to stay home."

"No, it's okay," Cam said immediately—just as I'd known he would. "I don't mind, if you're sure *you* won't feel weird about it." He smiled and squeezed my hand. "You know, me out with another woman . . ."

Okay, so maybe I was already feeling a teensy bit weird. But I wasn't about to let *him* see that. Instead, I just waved one hand airily.

"Don't give that a second thought," I assured him. "It's totally cool with me. Listen, I'd better get back home before

Mom notices I didn't load the dishwasher yet. Here's Jaylene's number. I'll have Allie tell her you'll call."

I pulled my hand away from his and dug into my pocket for the paper with Jaylene's phone number on it. Tossing it at him, I hurried off before either of us could change our minds.

The next week flew by. I was so busy with all the usual stuff that I hardly had time to obsess over Cam's Big Date. Well, not more than an hour or two a day, anyway. Allie had promised to fill me in as soon as she heard from Jaylene, and she showed up at my house bright and early on Saturday morning.

I hustled her upstairs before my father could spot her. Dad was busy typing up the notes from the latest Christmas Ball committee meeting on the den computer, and I knew he was probably looking for any excuse to take a break. If he spotted Allie, he was likely to start some long-winded discussion about how the Packers were doing this year. Allie was a casual football fan at best, but since Mom and I had no interest at all, Dad would take whatever he could get. And I didn't want to waste any time before getting the scoop.

"Well?" I asked as soon as we were safely in my room. "Did you talk to her?"

"Uh-huh." Allie wandered over to my desk and picked up the framed photo of Cam and me that stood there. "Have you talked to Cam yet?"

I shook my head. "Mom's been on the landline for the past hour, and my cell is recharging. So spill! Was it a total disaster, or did they both survive the experience?"

"Well, Jaylene said that Cam was a total gentleman last night."

"Yeah. Big surprise there." The cat was sleeping on my bed. I carefully pushed her over so I could sit down. "Did she mean it as a compliment or an insult?" I grinned. "I'm not sure Jaylene would appreciate the gentlemanly type."

"Think again," Allie said. "Actually, she told me she thinks Cam looks supersexy in a suit and tie."

"She's right. He does."

I suddenly felt a flash of concern. What if Jaylene really fell for Cam—and why wouldn't she?—while he was just being polite? I hadn't really considered that possibility. I didn't know Jaylene all that well, but I certainly hadn't intended to break her heart or anything. I also hadn't wanted to complicate Cam's life by forcing him to deal with that kind of awkward situation.

"So, did she say anything about how the two of them, you know, got along?" I asked.

Allie nodded. "She's convinced that Cam really got a kick out of her, um, out-there personality. And her, you know, *earthy* sense of humor."

"Really?"

"Really. Apparently they stopped off somewhere for coffee after the banquet and talked for over an hour." She took a deep breath. "Basically, Lex, it sounds like they *both* had a really great time."

Five

I have to admit it, I was stunned. For a while there, I'd started to assume that my little get-Cam-a-new-girlfriend project could take all year.

But I shook it off. After all, this was exactly what I'd wanted. Okay, so maybe I hadn't expected it to happen right now, or with this particular girl. Then again, Alexander Fleming probably hadn't expected to discover penicillin when he'd noticed that mold in his petri dish. And just look how that turned out.

"That's great!" I told Allie. "If they really do like each other, that means it's time for the *real* work to begin. It's not like Cam is just going to suddenly kick me to the curb because a cute girl smiled at him and he kinda liked it." I shook my head fondly. Gentlemanly indeed! "No, we're definitely going to have to push this along if we want it to have any chance of sticking."

"What do you mean, *we*?" Allie frowned. "Uh-uh, no way. Don't include me in that. I did my part by setting up the Jaylene thing, and I feel weird enough about that."

"Okay, chill. You're right; you did your part. You're off the hook for the rest." I knew that if push came to shove, she'd back me up on whatever I needed. That was what friends were for. But she was such an incurable romantic that I knew I shouldn't be surprised if she wasn't exactly jumping for joy at the thought of helping Cam move on.

She nodded, then cleared her throat. "Um, so what do you have in mind, anyway?" she asked cautiously.

I held back a smile. Allie was incurably curious, too.

"Well, I hadn't really thought about it yet," I said, my mind already clicking into high gear as it worked through the next stage of this plan. "But Cam already volunteered to be on Mom's food committee. So I guess I can start by getting Jaylene on the committee too, so they'll have to spend lots of time together. . . ."

Nick swung the roll of snowflake-print wrapping paper like a golf club, connecting with a pudgy little tube of silver ribbon and sending it flying into the rec room wall with a solid *thwack*. He nodded with satisfaction as the ribbon unraveled its way to the floor, then turned to face me.

"Okay, let me get this straight," he said. "You want me to have a man-to-man talk with Cam about how he should dump you?"

"Sort of." I tied off the bow on the empty box I'd just finished wrapping. Nick and I were supposed to be working on the fake gifts that would go under the town's Christmas tree, though he wasn't working on them very hard at the moment. "You'll need to be way more subtle about it than that. Just remind him that he should never be afraid to go for what he wants or do what's best for him. That kind of thing. You know, guy stuff."

"Yeah." Nick snorted. "Guy stuff. Got

it. 'Cause we guys just love a nice chat about relationships and feelings and that sort of thing. Maybe we can sip some chamomile tea and have our nails done while we discuss it."

I grinned. "Hey, whatever works for you. Remember, this is all for Cam's own good." I set my gift-wrapped package aside and reached for another box. "I've been dropping hints for the past week and a half since their date, so your little chat is just a way to make him think about things so he can't blow it off and pretend nothing's different."

"Hints? What kind of hints?"

I shrugged. "You know. Mentioning how I hope that whatever happens with college and stuff next year, we'll always stay friends. Turning my head or coughing whenever he looks like he's thinking about kissing me. That sort of thing." I took a deep breath. "And tonight, I'm going to call and cancel on him for next Friday. I'll tell him I need the time to finish up the last of my applications or something."

"What?" Nick looked startled. "You mean you're backing out of your traditional day-after-Thanksgiving date?"

I wasn't surprised by his reaction. Over the past three years, Leftover Turkey Day had been sacrosanct. Cam and I always spent the entire afternoon eating cold turkey sandwiches, snuggling on the couch watching movies, and just enjoying each other's company.

"Yeah. I have to." I sighed. It wasn't going to be easy to purposely miss my last chance at that particular tradition. But what choice did I have? "Blowing him off for Leftover Turkey Day is guaranteed to get his attention even if nothing else does."

Sure enough, Cam sounded shocked when I called him to pull out of our post-Thanksgiving date. "You're joking, right?" he said, sounding so plaintive that I almost changed my mind about the whole thing. "But we always get together for Leftover Turkey Day."

"I know." I clenched the phone tightly, glad that I hadn't tried to do this in person. "I'm really sorry. But maybe a rain check? Say, Saturday night? I should definitely be all finished by then. We could go see the Candy Cane Carolers concert down by the lake."

"Um, all right. Saturday night it is, then." There was a long pause. "Good luck with those apps." Cam still sounded disappointed and a little confused. Most guys probably would have pointed out that I could have planned to finish my applications on Saturday night instead so we could keep our Friday-afternoon date. But Cam wasn't most guys; he knew me too well. He probably assumed I had the application process planned out down to the minute. And he was far too caring and respectful to ask me to change that just in the name of tradition.

"Great, thanks. You're so understanding, Cam. A really good friend," I said. "That's the thing I've always appreciated about you the most, you know. Your friendship."

"Uh-huh, me too. Listen, maybe on Saturday we can talk about our costume for the Ball," he said. "Nick and I were talking the other day and I asked him to pick up the reindeer costume just in case, but if you don't want to do that, then we only have a month left to figure something out. And you know the good ones always go early. . . ."

"Sure, maybe. There are a few things we should probably talk about on Saturday, actually. Oops! I think I hear Mom calling me. Gotta go."

I hung up quickly. Whew! That had been harder than I'd expected. Images were flashing through my mind—me and Cam laughing over leftover turkey last year, and the year before, and the year before that . . . Me and Cam dancing together at the Ball last year, and the year before, and the year before that . . .

But I did my best to push all that aside as I picked up the phone again. Reaching into my pocket, I pulled out Jaylene's number and then dialed. When she answered, I took a deep breath.

"Jaylene, hi!" I said cheerfully. "It's Lexi Michaels. Listen, what do you have planned for Saturday night?"

And just like that, the deed was done. I arranged for Jaylene to attend that Saturday night concert as well, convincing her that a very special surprise blind date would be meeting her there. The annual Carolers show was pretty informal—just bleacher seating on the lawn in Lakeside Park near the ice-skating inlet. I figured Cam and Jaylene would spot each other once they were both there. Like I said, Jaylene tends to be pretty hard to miss.

Still, I was a bundle of nerves as I paced back and forth across my room, watching the clock hanging over my desk. It was six forty-eight. The concert started at seven.

Allie was there too, lying on my green checkered bedspread, tickling Blitzen under the chin. That cat hated just about everyone and everything else in the world, but she always tolerated anything Allie did to her, even breaking out in a raspy purr once in a while.

"There's still time to change your mind, you know," Allie said. "You could call and tell Cam you're running late. Then we could go down there, explain to Jaylene that her date got held up . . ."

I shook my head. "I've come this far. I can't wimp out now."

Taking a deep breath to settle the squirrels doing backflips in my stomach, I picked up the phone and hit the speed dial button for Cam's number. He answered on the second ring.

"Lexi? Is that you? Where are you?"

"Cam!" I shot a glance at Allie. For half a second I was tempted to take her advice and change my mind. But I fought the feeling. This was for the best. For *both* of us. "Um, are you at the lake?"

"Of course. The show starts in, like, five minutes. Are you on your way?"

"Not exactly. I'm so sorry, Cam. I don't think I can make it tonight after all. Something came up."

"Are you serious? You're not coming?" It takes a lot to irritate Cam, but I thought I detected a note of irritation in his voice now. I certainly couldn't blame him—I hadn't exactly been Girlfriend of the Year lately—but it still made me feel kind of bad.

"Sorry," I said again. "Um, I have to go. I'll explain later. Sorry."

When I hung up, Allie was staring at me with a frown. "So that's it?" she said. "That's your great master plan? What if he just decides to leave?"

"He won't." I set down the phone and collapsed into my desk chair. "By now the singers will be setting up. He won't want to leave in front of them—it would be rude."

Allie couldn't argue with that. She's known Cam a long time.

"Okay," she said. "But how do you know he'll end up hanging out with Jaylene just 'cause you stood him up? There are probably lots of other people there he could hang out with instead."

"She's not exactly the bashful type, remember? Even if she doesn't end up assuming he's her blind date, she's sure to spot him and go over and say hi, especially after all the time they've been spending together lately on the food committee and everything." I grabbed the phone again. "Besides, I have a spy there to make sure it all happens like it should." I hit a different speed dial button.

"Yo," a familiar voice answered. "Lex? Mission accomplished. Was that you who called him a minute ago? I saw him answer his cell."

"It was me." I mouthed Nick's name at Allie to let her know who was on the line. "So he's with Jaylene now?"

"Uh-huh. She spotted him as soon as she came in and made a beeline straight for him. They've been sitting together for, like, ten minutes."

"Great. So where are you? You have to make sure Cam doesn't spot you, or he'll definitely invite you to hang with them, or—"

"Relax, Lexi." Nick chuckled into the phone. "Leave that to me," he added, lowering his voice and putting on an atrocious attempt at a British accent. "Remember, I am Michaels. *Nick* Michaels."

"What?" Allie whispered as I rolled my eyes. "What's he saying?"

"In case you haven't noticed, my dear cousin is actually a ten-year-old boy," I told her. "He's living out his James Bond fantasies."

"Hey, who are you talking to?" Nick asked.

"Just Allie," I said into the phone. "Listen, call me if anything happens, okay? I'll be here all night."

"Ten four." Nick hung up, and I did the same.

Allie still looked kind of confused. "So I still don't get why Jaylene would assume that Cam's her date," she said. "I thought you convinced her you'd set her up with some hot mystery guy."

"Right. But I dropped just enough hints for her to assume that guy might be Cam."

This had been the trickiest part of the plan. Jaylene knew that Cam and I were a couple, of course. But I was counting on the fact that she hadn't been around long enough—or paid enough attention—to realize just how serious a couple we were.

This was how I'd figured it would go. Thanks to my hints and the lack of other eligible guys wearing a striped scarf at the concert, Jaylene would think that Cam was her mystery date and assume that I'd set the two of them up on purpose. If I knew Cam—and I did—he would figure out the mistake quickly, but would be far too polite to tell Jaylene the truth. He would naturally assume that she'd been stood up by her real date and wouldn't want her to feel hurt and rejected. Besides, there wouldn't be much time for explanations before the concert started.

So he would play along, planning to figure out a way to let her down easy at the end of the evening. But Jaylene liked Cam—I already knew that. And she wasn't the least bit shy. . . . If she assumed I'd set them up on purpose, I figured that the good feelings left over from their earlier "date," along with the friendship they were building on the food committee, would take care of the rest. It was sort of like mixing chemicals in chem lab. If you put the right ones together in exactly the right proportions, you got the result you wanted.

Now all I could do was sit and wait to see whether or not I'd measured those chemicals right.

Nick finally called at around ten thirty. I'd forced Allie to stay and help keep me distracted from what might or might not be going on down at the concert. We'd spent the first part of the evening working on her college essays, and when she'd gotten bored with that we'd switched to listening to music and then to playing Monopoly. When the phone rang, I jumped up so fast that I knocked the game board off the bed. Playing pieces, dice, and fake money scattered everywhere. Blitzen, who had been napping on the rug, woke up just long enough to bat the thimble under the bed.

"Nick?" I said into the phone. "Is that you?"

"It's me." He sounded weirdly somber. "I can't believe it, Lexi. I mean, I know you can do anything you set your mind to. But

I can't believe you actually pulled this off. It's almost kind of . . . I don't know, *eerie*."

My stomach did a funny little loop-de-loop. "What?" I demanded. "What happened?"

"It was just like you predicted," he said. "They sat together for the concert."

"And?" I prompted.

Even through the phone, I heard him take a deep breath. "Well, you know that Jaylene chick isn't, you know, the bashful type," he said. "Plus it's pretty cold out here tonight, and I think she's still wearing her Georgia wardrobe. So she started, like, snuggling up to Cam about halfway through. And she sort of grabbed his arm and put it around her, and he left it there."

I winced. Yeah, it was what I had wanted to happen, more or less. That didn't make it any easier to hear. Or to imagine.

"What?" Allie whispered, clearly reading the expression on my face.

"He was probably just afraid she'd freeze to death," Nick added quickly. "Like I said, her jacket wasn't really the kind of thing most people would wear to sit around outside in Wisconsin at the end of November. And her skirt was pretty short too, so her legs were . . . Well, anyway. They didn't actually kiss or anything like that. At least not that I saw. But they were both laughing and talking when they were walking out just now, and she kept kind of squeezing his arm . . ."

"I get the picture." I didn't particularly want to hear any more details. "Thanks, Nick. Now I guess I just have to wait and see what happens next. I've done what I could—it's up to Cam now."

I hung up and told Allie what Nick had reported. She looked stricken. "Oh, Lexi," she cried. "I'm sorry!"

"Don't be." I steeled myself, doing my best to get the big picture back in focus. "This is what has to happen, remember? It's the best thing—for everyone."

On Sunday morning, Cam turned up on my doorstep bright and early. His face was haggard and conflicted, and the deep shadows under his eyes made me wonder if he'd slept at all.

"Lexi," he blurted out. "We need to talk."

"Come on in." I stepped back, and he followed me into the foyer. Luckily my parents were both out, so we had the house to ourselves. "What's up?"

He took a deep breath. "Last night," he blurted out. "Um, the concert?"

I could tell this wasn't easy for him. "Uh-huh," I said. "Did you stay and watch? Did you run into anyone you knew there?"

"As a matter of fact, I did." The words came slowly, as if each one had to be dragged up out of his toes with a rusty fish-hook. "Um, it was that girl Jaylene? You know, from the banquet? And the food committee?"

"Oh, sure!" I said, doing my best to sound normal. As if I didn't know what was coming. I had to be strong—for both of us. "She seems really cool. And you guys have been getting along really well on that committee, right?"

"Yeah. And actually, we—we sort of got along pretty well last night, too." He gulped, his face turning red. "I think she, you know, likes me. And—and you and I . . . well, I feel like we haven't really been communicating lately. Like you're not that into, you know, *us* anymore."

"Oh." I forced myself to stop there. I didn't want to throw him off.

"So anyway, I was thinking." He paused and took another deep breath. "What do you think if we, you know, take a break for a while. See other people? I—I think that might be for the best, you know? What do you think?"

He gazed at me with those earnest, puppy-dog eyes of his, and I almost lost it. Yes, he was kind of digging Jaylene right now. And no wonder. She was fun-loving and interested and available. All the things I *hadn't* been lately.

But I knew Cam well enough to tell that he believed that maybe this was what I wanted, and that he wanted to save me from having to do it. I also suspected that all it would take was for me to tell him that it *wasn't* what I wanted, and Jaylene would be out of the picture just like that.

But I didn't say it. I couldn't let myself. If I backed down now, all the hard, painful work I'd done would be for nothing. And nothing would have changed. The facts would still be what they were. I couldn't let my emotions overcome logic.

"You may be right, Cam," I said softly, not quite daring to meet his eye. "Things haven't been the same between us lately.

And I understand. I really do. We can still be friends, right?"

"Of course!" His hand twitched, as if he'd started to reach out to me and then caught himself. I pretended not to notice.

"Great." I made my smile as sincere as possible. "That's the important part anyway, right? So consider us officially friends from now on, okay? And as a friend, I hope you and Jaylene will be really happy together. Really."

Six

After Cam left I had that same sort of breathless, almost out-of-body feeling I always got whenever I aced a big test or won an academic award. Cam always jokingly called it the "rush of success."

This time, though, it was undercut with a feeling of sadness. Even more than I'd expected, actually. It had been a good four years—*really* good—and it was hard to believe it was over. But I tried not to dwell on that. Instead, I focused on the positive. That rush. I'd done it, against all odds! Now I could relax and look forward to the future without the constant, nagging worry over what would become of us next year. I could stop worrying about hurting Cam and know that he was going to be okay.

Allie let out a wail when I called and told her. "I can't believe he did it!" she cried. "I never thought this would actually happen. I mean, I know you said it was going to happen, and so I believe it because you're usually right about stuff. But still, I never thought it would actually happen!"

"I know. You're a hopeless romantic," I said. "But this is all for the best. You'll see."

"Hmm." She didn't sound convinced. "So what now?"

"What do you mean?"

"Are you going to start dating right away?"

I hadn't really thought about that. "I guess there's no reason to wait," I said. "I mean, Cam already has someone. Knowing him, he'll probably feel all guilty and weird if he thinks I might be lonely without him." I nodded, switching the phone to my other hand. "You know, you're right, Allie. That's very logical of you! I definitely should start dating other people right away."

"That's not what I meant," she protested. Then she sighed. "Okay. But don't forget about the Rebound Guy Theory."

"Remind me on that one?"

"Your rebound guy should be someone as different as possible from your ex," she said. Then she sniffled. "I can't believe Cam is now your *ex*. . . ."

"Focus, Allie!"

"Okay, sorry. Anyway, so Mr. Rebound should be totally different, but nobody you would ever be serious about long-term. He's like the palate-cleansing sorbet you have between the courses of a good meal."

I laughed. She really did have a way with words sometimes. Maybe she'd make that bestselling book happen after all.

"Okay," I said. "Well, if you think of anyone that fits the bill, let me know. I'm a little rusty on this whole dating deal. I mean, the last time I went out with anyone but Cam, I still had a nine thirty curfew, and a peck on the lips at the end of a date was cause for gossip and scandal."

"Aw, that's true. You and Cam have been together for so long. Too bad it had to end now."

I rolled my eyes. "Look, I feel bad enough about this as it is," I said. "Enough with the guilt trip, okay?"

"Sorry." She sounded a bit wounded. "But I'm kind of glad to hear you admit that you feel bad. It's kind of hard to tell sometimes."

"Whatever." I didn't feel like getting in a fight with my best friend today of all days, even if she was practically accusing me of being a robot. "Sorry for snapping at you. I guess maybe I'm a little touchy right now."

She immediately sounded more sympathetic. "No, *I'm* sorry," she said. "You're allowed. I know this has to be rough—you know, getting dumped." She paused, then couldn't help adding, "Even if it was, you know, all your idea."

"Thanks." I smiled, knowing she was trying. "Listen, I should go call Nick and let him know."

"Okay. Call me if you need me."

I'd barely hit the button to hang up when the phone rang in my hand. "Hello?" I said.

"Lexi? Yo, it's me. Bruce. So I hear you're swinging single these days."

I winced. News travels fast in a small town. Still, Cam's buddy wasn't the first one I'd expected to call to offer his sympathies.

"Um, that's right," I told him. "As you

probably heard, Cam met someone else. I'm really happy for them."

"Cool. So you're over it already?" he said. "Then how about going out with me? You know what they say—you're supposed to get right back on the horse, right?"

I wasn't sure if that was one of his sleazy little jokes or just a bad choice of words. But it didn't really matter. Now that I thought about it, maybe I shouldn't have been so surprised to hear from Bruce. He'd been obviously lusting after me for years. I'd always thought he was at least half joking with all the little innuendos and lingering glances—after all, he'd never hesitated to do all that stuff right in front of Cam—but then again, maybe not. Okay, so maybe most guys probably wouldn't have asked me out within an hour of the breakup. But I'd always known that Bruce wasn't like most guys.

And maybe that was perfect. Allie's Rebound Guy Theory floated through my head, and I smiled. Complete opposite of my ex? Check. Nobody I'd ever be serious about? *Double* check.

"Sure, why not?" I said. "Sounds like fun."

"Great!" Bruce actually sounded a little surprised. "You won't regret this, Lexi. What should we do? Dinner? Dancing? A candlelit evening at my place?"

I shuddered. There was rebounding, and then there was *rebounding*. "I have a better idea," I said quickly. "How about the North Pole? The first is only a few days away."

December 1 at the North Pole Theater was another of Claus Lake's holiday traditions. That was always the date of the old-fashioned movie house's first annual showing of *It's a Wonderful Life*. The theater served eggnog and Christmas cookies in the lobby, the whole place was draped in tinsel, and a barbershop quartet provided the preshow entertainment. It was quite the Xmastravaganza.

"Okay, sure, whatever turns you on," Bruce agreed. "Pick you up at six thirty?"

"I'll be waiting with jingle bells on," I joked.

As soon as I hung up, I wondered if I'd just made a big mistake. Rebound Guy Theory or not, was it wrong to go out with someone just to help make sure my plan stuck? Especially someone like *Bruce*?

But my logical mind soon overruled the twinges of guilt. Bruce wasn't exactly the sensitive type, and he was certainly used to getting plenty of rejection from me. Yes, he was as good a way as any to ease my way back into the dating stream.

"Whoa, it's packed! I hope we can get a parking space." Bruce leaned forward and peered out through the windshield of his battered old Mustang.

I shot him a look. "Yeah, it's always like this on the first. Haven't you ever been before?"

"Nah. Not really my scene."

We were driving slowly toward the north end of Pine Street. Traffic was bumper to bumper with cars lined up to get into the old movie theater's parking lot. I glanced out the window as we drove past the building. There was a wreath draped on the big old-fashioned red-and-white barber pole out in front that had given the place its name. People were lined up on either side of the pole waiting to get in.

Unlike Bruce, I'd come to the North Pole on almost every December 1 of my life—the last three of them with Cam. It felt strange to be arriving with someone else.

We finally reached the alley leading back between the theater and the Laundromat next door. The narrow parking lot behind the buildings was almost full, but Bruce found a spot between a pickup truck and a tree.

"Here we are," he said, turning off the engine and looking around at the dozens of people hurrying toward the theater from all corners of the lot, most of them huddled inside heavy coats and parkas. "Along with half the town, looks like."

We climbed out of the car and joined the migration. A dusting of snow had fallen the day before and the weather was chilly and dry. The steamy air drifting into the parking lot from the back of the Laundromat hit my face like a damp washcloth, and I could almost feel my hair frizzing. And at that precise moment, I noticed a familiar green Volvo parked in the first row just behind the theater. Figured he'd arrived early enough for a good spot.

Bruce saw the car, too. "Hey, looks like Cam is here," he said. Then he glanced over at me. "Oops. *Awk*ward."

"It's no big deal." I pulled my gaze away from the car. "Cam and I are still friends. Anyway, like you said, half the town is here tonight."

"Whatever you say." Bruce put one hand on the small of my back to guide me around a puddle of snowy mush. I almost acted on instinct and slapped the hand away, but then I reminded myself that we were on a date. And he seemed to be trying to be a gentleman so far. Still, his touch felt oddly heavy and foreign even through my heavy wool coat.

I spotted Cam as soon as we rounded the corner. He was standing in front of the barber pole, digging into his pocket for something. Jaylene was beside him, clinging onto his arm and laughing. She looked cold in her fashionable little baby blue jacket.

I froze. The logical part of my mind knew that if Cam had broken up with me to be with Jaylene, that meant I was likely to see him, you know, *with* Jaylene. And considering the size of our town, that was bound to happen sooner rather than later.

But I still wasn't prepared for how it

felt. Seeing them together. Her hand on his arm, her cute little round face peering up at him. Him looking back at her and smiling. Cam. *My* Cam.

The logical portion of my brain struggled to regain control. It did its best to remind the other parts that Cam wasn't *mine* anymore. . . .

"You okay?" Bruce had dropped his hand from my back by now, but he stepped over and nudged me with one shoulder. "We could go do something else if you want. Grab some dinner or drive out to the mall to see a real movie."

"No, it's okay." I struggled to focus on the positive. This was what I wanted. My plan had worked. "Thanks. I'm fine. Come on, let's go say hi."

Cam saw us coming when we were still a few yards away. His whole face sort of crumpled, but then he forced a smile.

"Hey, guys," he called out. "What's up?"

Jaylene looked up too. "Lexi!" she exclaimed in her Southern accent, which made my name sound more like "Lakesie." Weirdly, she seemed genuinely happy to see me. Then again, maybe it wasn't so weird. After all, she thought I was the one who'd hooked her up with Cam. "Isn't this fun? Ah can't believe Ah'm about to see *It's a Wonderful Life* in a theater instead of on TV. Ya'll really know how to do Christmas around here, that's for sure!"

"Yeah, that's Claus Lake for you." I tried to return her smile sincerely. After all, this ridiculously awkward moment wasn't *her* fault. No, it was pretty much, well, *mine*. "Um, Jaylene, have you met Bruce?"

"Oh, sure thang. We had a nice chat when he came to pick up Cammie after one of our committee meetins last week." Jaylene snuggled up against Cam, one of her arms sneaking around his waist.

Cam smiled weakly. I could tell he was more than a little uncomfortable with Jaylene's public display of affection. That wasn't just because I was there, either. Cam hated that kind of touchy-feely stuff.

At least I thought he did. He didn't do a thing as Jaylene gave him a squeeze, then started playing with the sleeve of his coat. Maybe he was just too nice to protest and embarrass her. Or maybe he didn't mind it that much after all.

For one crazy second, I had the urge to leap forward and shove her away from him.

But I did my best to repress it, just repeating my mantra. This was all for the best. All for the best.

Wasn't it?

The next day was Saturday, and the mall was packed. The noise, smells, and body heat of hundreds of frenzied shoppers dashing among dozens of overstocked stores hit me as soon as I pushed in through the heavy glass doors. Everywhere I looked, bright red and green signs screamed about the fantastic holiday savings. But I ignored them all. I wasn't there to shop.

Dodging through the crowds, I headed for the high-end department store in the west wing of the mall. Allie had a part-time job there wrapping gifts for the holiday season. It paid better than being one of Santa's elves, as she'd done the previous year, and involved far fewer sticky little-kid hands and runny noses wiped on your shirt. Aside from those dubious advantages, it didn't look like much more fun to me.

"Lexi!" Allie looked up from wrapping a decorative candle for a bored-looking preteen boy and his father. Her dark hair was flopping in her face, totally uncontained by her perky candy-cane-striped headband, and her expression was frazzled. "Hi! What are you doing here?"

"Sorry to bother you at work. I was hoping to talk to you about something. But it looks like you're kind of busy, so . . ."

"Hold that thought." Allie finished her wrapping job with expert speed, handed the package to the boy, then checked her watch. "Hey, Rhonda!" she called to the stout gray-haired woman at the next table, "I'm going on break, okay?"

"You betcha." The woman barely glanced up from the picture frame she was encasing in sparkly silver paper. "But be back by the lunch rush, all right, hon?"

We hurried away from the gift wrap area. "So what do you want to talk about?" Allie asked curiously.

"I'll tell you in a second," I replied. "Want to go sit down? I'll buy you a coffee."

"Okay. I could use the caffeine." Allie fiddled with her hair while we walked, trying to get her headband to hold it back out of her face.

It was still early, and the food court was relatively quiet. It only took a few minutes to get our coffees from the doughnut stand.

Black with one sugar for me, and cream and three sugars for Allie. We found an empty table and sat down.

"I went to the North Pole with Bruce last night," I began.

"Oh, right." Allie wrinkled her nose. "How was it? Did he sprout eight extra hands as soon as the lights went down?"

"Well, sort of. But that's not what I wanted to talk to you about." I took a deep breath, wrapping my hands around my steaming coffee cup. "I ran into Cam there. With Jaylene."

"Oh, Lexi!" Allie exclaimed sympathetically. "Sorry. Was it totally weird?"

"Yeah. Weirder than I expected." I hesitated, not sure how to say what I wanted to say next. "You know, all this time I've been really sure I was doing the right thing. But last night, just for a second, well . . ."

Allie didn't even wait for me to finish. "So you're having second thoughts about this crazy breaking-up-with-Cam plan?" she exclaimed, bouncing in her seat so vigorously that she almost tipped over her coffee. "Oh my God, Lexi. I thought you'd never come to your senses!"

"Now, hold on," I said. "I'm not saying

I've changed my mind. Not really."

"But you have, haven't you?" She stopped bouncing and gripped the edge of the table, staring at me intensely. "You've got to do it, Lexi. Just this once, go with your heart instead of your brain. I'm sure you can still get Cam back. It's not too late—not yet."

She had a certain demented gleam in her eyes. I recognized that gleam. It meant she was in the midst of formulating a new theory.

"Okay, let's hear it," I said.

"What?"

"You know what. The theory." I raised an eyebrow at her. "You *do* have a theory that applies to this situation, don't you?"

She smiled. "As a matter of fact, I do. It's a new one. I'm thinking about calling it the Dozen Dates Theory." She tapped the stirrer from her coffee on the table. "See, I've sort of been thinking lately about how relationships get started. And how some of them last, and some don't. And just how important those early days are to a new couple as they get to know each other and stuff."

"Okay, Dr. Freudina," I said. "So what does this have to do with me and Cam?"

"I'm getting there. See, the idea behind the Dozen Dates Theory is that by the time a new couple has gone out a dozen times, their relationship is pretty much set." She shrugged. "There's more to it than that, of course. I mean, I'm thinking this one could make a whole book if I work it out right." She pushed her coffee aside and leaned forward. "But for your situation, Lex, the key point is this: You need to move fast."

"Huh? What do you mean?"

"I mean this is the grace period," she said. "The honeymoon. You know, for Cam and his new woman. That means you still have a chance to get him back. There's still time. But not much." She stared at me seriously. "Because if you let Cam and Jaylene get a dozen dates under their belts, that's it. You can kiss any hope of rekindling your own romance good-bye."

Seven

The Dozen Dates Theory sounded just about as wacky as the rest of Allie's long line of theories. But for once, I wasn't in the mood to pick it apart bit by unscientific bit.

"Two dates, twelve dates—it doesn't matter," I told her, shoving my coffee away. "I mean, this is what I wanted—Cam happy with someone else and me free to move on into the future without worrying about him. I just had a moment of weakness, that's all. You know, because of seeing them together like that. I'll just have to suck it up and get used to it."

Allie looked disappointed. "Wait, but I thought you said you weren't sure this was the right thing anymore. You should always go with your instincts."

"My instincts tell me to use my brain," I said. "And my brain has been telling me for months that I have to figure out a way to solve the problem of me and Cam before it's too late and we end up like Nick and Rachel."

"That would never happen to you guys," she insisted. "It only happened to them because of Rachel deciding she didn't want to bother with a long-distance relationship."

I stared at her, suddenly feeling as if we were speaking different languages. Specifically, I was speaking Logic and she was, as usual, fluent in Ridiculously Impractical Emotion. How many times did I have to point out the facts to her? It felt as if I were trying to convince her that two trains heading in opposite directions were totally safe, while she kept insisting hysterically that they were sure to crash into each other at any moment.

Thinking about that made me feel a little more settled. I was just going to have to get a handle on my emotions for a while—just until I got used to the new world order. Seeing Cam with Jaylene would get easier with time and exposure. It had to.

"Thanks for talking it through with me," I told Allie, sitting back in my seat. "I think I'm back on track now. Even your Dozen Dates Theory helped."

"Really?" She looked hopeful. "You mean it helped you see that you've got to get back together with Cam before it's too late?"

I shook my head. "I mean it helped me see that I only have to wait them out for, like, nine more dates before I can stop worrying about Cam. You know, if we count that banquet and the concert as their first two dates, and then the movie as number three."

She looked disappointed. "But—"

"So!" I interrupted brightly, deciding we could both benefit from a change of subject. "Any progress on your own love life lately? Sorry I've been so wrapped up in my own thing that I haven't asked."

"It's okay. And not really." She glanced at her watch. "But listen, let's talk about that later, all right? I'd better head back now."

I walked Allie back to work, then browsed through the department store for a few minutes looking for gift ideas for my family. But I couldn't seem to focus on the cases and shelves full of jewelry and clothes and perfume and everything else under the sun. Finally I gave it up and headed back toward the mall.

I was still deep in thought as I stepped out of the hushed, tasteful interior of the department store back into the din of hurrying feet, screaming kids, and the Muzak version of "I Saw Mommy Kissing Santa Claus." It was a moment before my ears adjusted and I realized that someone was calling my name.

To my surprise, it was Andrew Cole. He had just stepped out of Radio Shack holding a shopping bag. His polished leather loafers squeaked on the tile floor as he hurried toward me.

"Lexi, hi," he said, straightening the collar of his long-sleeved polo. "Doing a little shopping?"

"Something like that." I tried to remember the last time Andrew and I had spoken to each other. Despite having been in most of the same classes for the past twelve years, we weren't what you'd call close, except maybe in the way that the

Green Bay Packers and the Chicago Bears could be considered close. To put it another way, we'd been fierce academic rivals since before either of us could spell *fierce academic rivals*.

"Hey, I was sorry to hear about you and Cam splitting up," Andrew said. "Uh, but I heard you're already dating again."

Oh, great. So Bruce was already bragging about that. I wondered what exactly he'd been telling people. Then again, knowing Bruce, I probably didn't want to know.

"Yeah, sort of, I guess," I said, drifting into a private little fantasy of shoving Bruce's wandering hands up his own butt.

"Great. Then how about we go out sometime?"

That snapped me back to reality. "What?" I blurted out. "Uh, we? You mean you and me? Going out on a date?"

"Sure, why not?" Andrew shrugged. His lower lip was twitching slightly. "Hope it's not too soon. I just don't want to miss my chance again."

"Again?"

He winced, looking as if he wished he could take it back. "Well, yeah," he admitted. "I thought about asking you out once before. Back in eighth grade. I wanted to ask you to the Christmas Ball, but you and Cam got together before I could."

Wow. That was so out of the blue I didn't know what to say for a second.

"Um, okay," I said at last. "Sure. That would be . . . nice."

"Great! Are you free tonight? How about dinner at Manfredi's?" Weirdly, he had that same triumphant gleam in his eye that he got on the rare occasion he received a higher grade than me on a test. I could only imagine what kind of theory Allie would come up with to explain that.

"Sounds good," I said, trying to sound normal. "I love that place."

"Fantastic. I'll pick you up at six."

You could call it bad luck. You could call it a statistical improbability. Or you could just call it what it was—life in a small town. Whatever the terminology, I could hardly believe my eyes when Andrew and I walked into Manfredi's that evening and I saw Cam and Jaylene sitting at one of the tables for two along the cozy little restaurant's back wall.

Date number four, I thought, Allie's

Dozen Dates Theory flitting across my mind. *But who's counting?*

Cam looked up and spotted me. He froze in midchew. I didn't have to look to see what he was eating: fettuccine carbonara. That was what he always ordered at Manfredi's.

We stared at each other for a second. Then his expression relaxed into sort of a sad smile. He lifted one hand in a wave, and I waved back, feeling as awkward as humanly possible. I mean, what were the odds? Even in Claus Lake? I was still waving when Jaylene glanced around curiously. She waved back cheerfully, then leaned forward to say something to Cam.

Andrew had just turned after giving our name to the maître d'. Following my gaze, he took in the sight of the happy couple. I had to hand it to him—he was as cool as a cucumber. Only a slight twitch of the lower lip gave away that he'd noticed anything. Without acknowledging the situation at all, he reached out and put an arm around my shoulders.

"Come on, Lexi," he said. "I think our table is ready."

I was so distracted as we walked across the tightly packed restaurant that I'm surprised I didn't trip over a table leg and land in someone's soup. When we reached our table by the front window, the maître d' stepped forward as if to pull out one of the chairs for me. But Andrew blocked him neatly, steering me to the other chair—the one with no view of Cam's table.

"Uh, thanks," I mumbled, still trying to wrap my head around what was happening here. Was I doomed to spend the rest of my senior year running into Cam and Jaylene everywhere I went? And if so, would it ever get easier to see them together?

I lurched into my seat, somehow managing to half miss and almost fall on my butt. Putting out my right arm to catch my balance, I accidentally set it down right on the lit candle in the center of the table.

"Ow!" I yelped, yanking my hand away from the flame and in the process almost falling off my chair again. Smooth. Really smooth. This was rapidly turning into a how-not-to manual for making a sexy impression on a first date with a new guy. Not to mention playing it cool in front of an ex and his new squeeze. Too bad Allie wasn't there—she could have been taking notes for her next bestseller.

My face burned as several nearby diners glanced over in surprise and Andrew stared at me as if I'd just sprouted a second head. He reached out and righted the candle before it could set the little holly-and-ivy wreath surrounding it aflame.

"Are you all right?" he asked.

"Fine." I stuck my singed finger in my mouth to soothe the burn. Then, realizing that wasn't helping make me look any more sophisticated or in control of the situation, I quickly removed it and surreptitiously wiped it on my pants beneath the table.

Fortunately the waitress appeared at that moment with a pitcher of ice water and our menus. I was able to hide my face behind the menu until I felt my cheeks start to return to their normal color.

Somehow, I survived the next half hour or so. I even managed to avoid peeking over my shoulder to see what Cam and Jaylene were doing. The trouble was, I couldn't seem to control my mind nearly as well. It kept drifting away from whatever Andrew was saying. Not that you could blame me too much for that. The guy only had one topic of conversation: himself. His choice of colleges. His predicted SAT score. His grades and extracurriculars. Oh, sure, once in a while he interrupted his autobiographical lecture to ask me a question about myself. I would grunt out some distracted, monosyllabic response, and then the Story of Andrew would continue. Of course, there *was* that one totally awkward moment when he mentioned something about wondering when the Simpson Scholarship would be announced already and then caught himself and stopped talking abruptly, apparently remembering that his primary competition for said scholarship was sitting across the table from him. His cheeks had sprouted little red spots for a moment, then he'd shrugged and changed the subject. Back to himself, of course.

I was relieved when he excused himself to go to the restroom. As soon as he was gone, I slumped in my seat and stared at my burned finger. It still stung a little and looked kind of red. I hoped it wouldn't swell up and make it hard to type. I still had a few applications to finish.

"Lexi?"

I glanced up, but I already knew who I'd see standing there beside the table.

I'd recognize that voice anywhere.

"Oh—hi, Cam," I said, quickly tucking my finger away out of sight within my fist. "Having a nice time?"

This time I couldn't resist glancing over my shoulder at his table. Jaylene was nowhere in sight.

He saw where I was looking. "Jaylene just went to the bathroom," he said. "Um, I mean the little girls' room." He smiled faintly. "That's what she calls it."

"Cute." I wasn't really in the mood to hear every little adorable thing about Jaylene. But I did my best to keep smiling as if it didn't bother me in the least.

"Anyway, I just wanted to come over and make sure you're okay." Cam gestured toward my hand. "It looked like you burned yourself pretty good."

"Oh." I was touched. "Yeah. I'll be all right. Thanks."

"You sure? Good." He looked down at my plate. If he noticed I'd barely touched my food, he didn't say anything. "Having the tortellini, huh? That's one of your favorites."

"Yeah. And let me guess—you got your usual fettuccine?"

"Believe it or not, no," he said with a

slightly sheepish laugh. "Jaylene talked me into trying the lasagna." He shrugged. "It's pretty good. Maybe not as good as the fettuccine, but good."

"Oh." Were we still talking about Italian food? I wasn't quite sure.

Cam shot a glance across the restaurant, suddenly looking a little uncomfortable. "Well, I'd better get back. Enjoy the rest of your dinner. And I hope your hand feels better too."

"Thanks."

He headed back to his seat. I watched him weave his way among the other tables. What a nice guy! Everyone always said that about him, of course, myself included. But until that moment, I wasn't sure I'd ever stopped to think about what the phrase *really* meant.

"I'm back!" Andrew announced as he returned to our table a minute or two later. He sat down and reached for his water glass. "So where were we? Oh yeah—I was just telling you about that weird essay question for the application to . . ."

I pasted a smile on my face and stared at him, still lost in the thoughts Cam's little visit had brought up. Andrew was exactly the kind of guy I probably *should* be with. He was smart and driven and likely to succeed and all sorts of other things I generally admired.

But was he "nice"? No, not really. Not like Cam.

A few minutes later Cam and Jaylene finished their meal and got up to leave. I watched them out of the corner of my eye as he retrieved her silly little baby blue coat from the hooks near the door and helped her put it on. As she fussed with her blond hair, pulling it out from beneath her fur-lined collar, Cam glanced over and saw me looking. He smiled and waved. I returned the smile weakly and wriggled my fingers in return.

"What are you looking at, Lexi?" Andrew interrupted himself. He looked over just in time to see Cam open the door for Jaylene. "Oh." He shrugged, then shoveled in a mouthful of lasagna before returning to his favorite topic. "So anyway, like I was saying, the admissions guy from Northwestern . . ."

As the door swung shut behind the happy couple, I picked up my fork and poked at my pasta, feeling a little sick. Would this ever get any easier?

I couldn't resist peeking out the window as Cam and Jaylene emerged onto the sidewalk just outside. She said something. He laughed and put his arm around her. She snuggled up to him, her little white mittens sneaking their way around his waist. Smile, smile, kiss . . .

And this is where we came in. Their spontaneous, romantic kiss hit me like a punch to the gut. What had I been thinking all these weeks? All this time, the idea of Cam—*my* Cam—with another girl had seemed somehow speculative and theoretical. Like a science hypothesis waiting to be proved or one of Allie's crazy theories being tested in a double-blind study.

But now that the result was standing right there in front of me, kissing on a snowy evening beneath the twinkling holiday lights, I somewhat belatedly realized the truth.

I was still in love with Cam.

Yep, there was no denying it any longer. Stuck in a rut, opposites attract and all, I still loved him. All the logic in the world couldn't change that. Which meant, of course, that I'd just made the stupidest mistake of my life.

Was it too late to fix it?

Eight

I'm not sure how I survived the rest of my date with Andrew. For one thing, I was already calling him Annoying Andrew in my head—I had to be really careful not to slip and say it out loud. Somehow, I didn't think he would have the sense of humor to handle something like that very well.

But that was far from my worst problem. Being with Andrew, and with Bruce before him, had only showed me what I would be missing if I couldn't figure out how to make things right with Cam. Okay, so maybe that spark had faded a bit over the years between Cam and me. But I couldn't imagine ever feeling the spark at all with those two guys. Or with anyone else, for that matter.

No, the grass definitely wasn't greener for me. But what about for Cam? Based on that kiss I'd just witnessed, I wasn't too sure.

"Here we are." Andrew pulled to a stop at the curb in front of my house. As I unhooked my seat belt, he leaped out of the car and raced around the front of it like a demented rabbit, slipping a little on the rapidly freezing slush on the road. Then he opened my door with a flourish.

"Thanks," I said, climbing out without taking the hand he held out to help me. I didn't want to give him any ideas.

Unfortunately, he already seemed to have them. After he'd closed the car door behind me, he hurried to catch up as I headed up the front walk. He slung one arm around my shoulders, squeezing a bit.

I resisted the urge to elbow him in the ribs. Instead, I waited until we reached the porch steps and then scooted up them quickly, managing to extricate myself from his arm in the process. He was a smart guy, and I hoped he'd take the hint.

But no. He climbed the steps after me and watched as I fished my house key out of my purse. My mind wandered back to a similar but oh-so-different wintry evening about four years earlier. Cam and I had just returned from our first real date—skating on the lake—and I'd been digging in my coat pocket for my key. It had been an amazing evening, and I hadn't wanted it to end. Cam and I had skated and talked and laughed and had a great time. I still remembered the tingle I'd felt, even through my wool gloves, when he'd shyly reached over to hold my hand as we'd glided along side by side across the ice and everything had felt so romantic and new. . . .

"This was fun," Andrew said, snapping me back to the here and now. "We should do it again sometime."

"Sure, maybe." I finally found the key and pulled it out. "Although with the holidays and all, I'm sure we'll both be kind of busy, right? Anyway, thanks for dinner."

"You're very welcome."

I glanced up to say good-bye. My eyes widened in alarm as I saw his eyes sort of squeeze half-shut and his lips go all poofy and start moving toward me like a heat-seeking missile. Yeah, so much for picking up my hints. He was going in for the good-night kiss.

I quickly turned my head, deflecting

him just in time. The kiss landed on my cheek instead of its intended target.

"Well, good night, then," I said as cheerfully as I could manage, stepping back and reaching for the door.

He opened his eyes and licked his lips, looking startled. "Oh," he said. "Um . . ."

But I didn't wait around to hear any more. Quickly stepping inside, I shut the door behind me without looking back.

The next day my mom asked me to run out to the mall to pick up some stuff she needed for her next food committee meeting. While I was there, I stopped in at the department store to see if Allie had time to talk. To my surprise, she wasn't there. Normally she worked every weekend day between Thanksgiving and Christmas Eve. The place was packed, and her coworkers were so frantic in their quest to wrap snowflake-print paper and curly red ribbons around everything in sight that I didn't even bother trying to ask them why Allie wasn't working. Instead, I just stopped off at her house on my way home.

"Hi, Lexi," Allie's mother greeted me when she opened the door. Mrs. Lin looked exactly like Allie would probably look in thirty years, right down to the tiny ponytail. "Nice to see you. Have you heard anything about that Simpson Scholarship yet? Allie tells me you'll probably win it this year."

"No, no word yet. You know how it is—Mrs. Simpson always likes to keep everyone in suspense for a while." I chuckled along with Mrs. Lin. "Um, is Allie home?"

"Oh, sure." She waved me inside. "She and Nick are in the den."

I blinked, a bit surprised to learn that my cousin was there. Allie and Nick hung out all the time, of course, but usually only when I was around. It was kind of like I was the oxygen atom in our water molecule of friendship.

"They're working on the decorations for the kiddie room at the Ball," Allie's mother added, ushering me toward the cozy den at the back of the house.

That explained it, then. Sure enough, when I entered the den it looked as if one of Santa's elves had exploded in there. Red and green paper scraps covered every available surface, from the burgundy carpet to the leather couch to Allie's shiny black hair. I wondered how Nick—or more likely, Nick's mom—had suckered her into helping with this one. Every year, while everyone over the age of twelve danced the night away in the main room, the younger kids gathered in the upstairs section of the fireman's hall under the supervision of a fleet of paid out-of-town babysitters for an evening of Christmas cookies, sing-alongs, naps, stories, tantrums, and games. They also had their own decorations up there, mostly consisting of paper garlands, Christmassy cutouts, and other nontoxic-if-eaten-or-licked items. Preparing that stuff for a bunch of sugar-hyped sprogs wasn't anyone's favorite task on the decorations committee.

Allie and Nick were bent over a sheet of construction paper together. They both looked up in surprise when I walked in and said hello.

"Lexi!" Allie exclaimed, jumping to her feet and brushing her hair out of her face. "What are you doing here? I mean, I was going to call you and see if you wanted to come help us with this stuff, but I figured you had that date last night and probably wanted to sleep in, plus I know you've got that last application essay to finish and then that paper for history class, so . . ."

She was babbling, probably out of sheer boredom. Or maybe the Elmer's glue had gone to her head. Either way, I brushed aside her torrent of explanations.

"I'm glad you guys are both here," I said. "I need to talk to you about something. It's important."

"Uh-oh," Nick joked. "The last time you said something like that, you'd decided to break up with Cam. Let me guess—this time you're breaking up with the two of us, right?"

"Very funny." Even though my mind was pretty much filled to capacity with my own problems, I couldn't help realizing that he sounded almost back to normal lately. At least Rachel hadn't broken him forever. "But I'm serious. I think I've made a colossal mistake."

Allie cocked her head. "Wait. Did you end up going out to dinner last night with Andrew?"

"Uh-huh." I'd scooted back into the department store the afternoon before to let her know about that invitation. "Let's just say it didn't go well. In more ways than one . . ."

Flopping down onto the leather sofa, I quickly filled them in on the whole evening. Nick let out a low whistle when I told them about seeing Cam and Jaylene at the restaurant, and Allie gasped with horror when I (briefly) described their kiss.

"So anyway," I finished, "I realize now that I was wrong. Cam is the guy for me. I never should have decided to end things with him." I took a deep breath. "So go ahead. Say it. You told me so, right?"

"Well, now that you mention it . . . ," Nick began.

Allie shut him up with a punch to the upper arm. "Don't," she said. "You know Lexi. She doesn't admit she's wrong very often, mostly because she *isn't* wrong very often. We don't want to make her feel any worse about being so, so, *so* wrong this time." She smiled at me. "But anyway, why are you here telling us about this? You should be at Cam's house right now getting back together with him!"

"What? It's not that simple."

"Sure it is," Nick urged, leaning back against the edge of an overstuffed armchair. "Cam's a reasonable guy. So you throw yourself at his feet, tell him you were an idiot, then kiss and make up."

Allie nodded vigorously. "Just be honest with him, and see if he'll consider trying again. I'm sure he will."

I sat up so fast that the sofa squeaked. "Are you insane? I can't tell him the truth about all the idiotic stuff I did to make this happen." I grimaced, feeling my cheeks go hot as I thought about all the deceptive tricks I'd pulled over the past couple of months. How could I have been such a fool? "He'd never understand," I added sadly. "He's so honest and straightforward—he'd probably never forgive or respect me ever again if he found out how I finagled the end of our relationship. Then I wouldn't even have him as a friend anymore, let alone anything more. And I *really* couldn't stand that."

"But you can't give up, Lexi!" Allie cried. "You have to get him back."

"Yeah," Nick said. "It's not like you to give up, Lex. That's why Dad always calls you the family go-getter."

"Don't worry, I'm not giving up," I told them. "I'm just saying I need to figure out the best way to handle this."

Allie looked dubious. "Well, you'd better hurry up and figure it out soon," she said. "Dozen Dates Theory, remember?"

Nick let out a snort. Clearly he'd heard about Allie's latest theory as well.

Allie shot him an irritated glance. "Anyway, I still think you can do it. Right now you've still got time on your side. See, I've been working out more of the theory lately, and there's something I'm calling the Nostalgia Footnote. That means that, as the recent ex, you still have the advantage of all the memories you two have together. But the closer you get to that dozen dates mark, the less weight that kind of thing—"

"Hold it," I interrupted, tapping my fingers on the arm of the sofa. "I think you might be on to something there with the nostalgia thing, Allie."

"Really?" She looked surprised and kind of delighted. And no wonder. That was probably the most enthusiastic response I'd ever given to one of her theories. "Well, I mean, sure I am. So if you just confess everything to Cam right now, his memories of your past together should totally overcome any weirdness about, you know, your methods."

"No, that's not what I mean." I leaned

forward and gazed thoughtfully at my cousin. "Hey Nick, I just realized your birthday's coming up in, like, a week."

"Let me guess. This is your way of warning me to expect an IOU instead of a real present again this year?"

Poor Nick was always getting shafted on the whole birthday-present thing. I guess that happens when your big day is too close to *the* big day. And like I said, in Claus Lake the entire autumn season is probably too close. Oh, and just in case it's not obvious, that's how Nick got his name. After all, being born in December in Claus Lake, what other name could he have?

"Don't worry," I told him. "Your birthday gift is already wrapped and waiting in a secret location in my house. But I was just thinking, shouldn't we all do something special to celebrate?"

He cocked one eyebrow suspiciously. "Why do I have the feeling this idea *isn't* coming from a genuine burst of cousinly love?"

"Of course it is." I grinned. "Then again, I've always been a multitasker, right? See, I was just thinking, how about if you invite the whole gang out ice-skating on the lake next weekend?"

"Hmm." Nick picked a sparkly bit of paper off his sleeve and flicked it across the room. "Could be fun, I guess. Plus that way nobody will be able to forget my birthday for once. But what's in it for you? You realize I'll have to invite Jaylene, too, right?"

I shrugged. "That's okay. She's from Georgia—she probably can't even skate. With any luck she'll spend most of her time drinking hot chocolate on shore and Cam and I can reminisce about the first time we went skating together."

"Ooh, I remember that." Allie smiled. "It sounded totally romantic."

"It was. So maybe being out there on the lake together will remind Cam of that night—you know, get that nostalgia thing working for me. If you guys are right and he wants me back too, that could be all it takes to kick-start a reconciliation—no messy confessions required." I shrugged. "If I play my cards right, Cam and I could be a couple again in plenty of time for the Ball. We can wear the funny front-and-back-halves-of-a-reindeer costume he picked out, and everything will be back to normal."

"Okay, what the hell. Let's do it," Nick said. "I'll start calling people tonight."

"Call Cam first, okay?" I urged. "There's not much point if he can't make it."

Nick snorted. "Right. No point at all."

Allie giggled. "Don't worry, Nick, she's crazed with jealousy—she doesn't know what she's saying." She turned to me. "But Lexi, even if this works, you're right back where you started. You know, that fabulous mismatched future you were so worried about before . . ."

That had been nagging at the back of my mind too. But I was trying to keep it back there for now.

"I know," I said. "But I'll just have to worry about that once I'm back with Cam."

Nine

"Brrr," Bruce complained. "Nick, dude, why'd you have to have your birthday at the coldest time of the year?"

"Don't be an idiot." I looked up from lacing my left skate, quickly tucking my bare fingers into my armpits in a vain attempt to thaw them enough to lace up the other skate. "If his birthday was in July, we wouldn't exactly be celebrating with an ice-skating party, would we?"

Still, he kind of had a point. It was cold. *Really* cold. Not that it's ever exactly balmy in Wisconsin in December, but it's usually not Siberia, either. But just my luck—a front had rolled in the night before and it was downright frigid, with a bitter wind gusting in and howling around the edges of the lake, shaking the latest snowfall off the tops of the pines. At the moment we were all still huddled around the benches and snow-covered pathways by the skating inlet, even though most of us had arrived at least ten or fifteen minutes earlier. Nobody seemed too eager to leave the relative shelter of the shoreline and hit the open ice.

But the weather wasn't the main reason I was feeling kind of tense. Cam hadn't even arrived yet, and I was already wondering if this had been a stupid idea. Nick hadn't been able to reach Cam on Sunday night. He'd tracked him down as soon as he could in school on Monday, but the best he'd been able to get from Cam was an "I'll let you know." Cam hadn't given him an answer until Tuesday morning, which meant Nick hadn't been able to start asking other people until after that. By then a large chunk of the guest list already had plans for Saturday afternoon. Then a few more had canceled because of the weather. Wimps.

So that left a pretty small group. Me. Nick. Allie. Bruce. Two giggly girls from Nick's music class. And finally, Cam and Jaylene—if they ever showed up. Now, normally Cam wasn't the type of guy to cancel at the last minute. If he committed to be somewhere, he was there, come hell, high water, or subzero windchill factor. But now that Jaylene was in the picture, I was starting to wonder if he was still as predictable as I'd always thought. After all, I never would have expected that impulsive, snowy kiss the other night, either. . . .

Ripping my mind away from that unwelcome image, I stood up, brushed some snow off my black Polartec pants, and surveyed our paltry group. When I'd come up with this idea, I'd envisioned Jaylene lost in crowds of people out on the ice, giving me free rein to zero in on Cam and work the nostalgia angle. After all, Nick had tons of friends, which meant his parties normally resembled New Year's Eve in Times Square. But with only eight of us, it wasn't going to be so easy to cut Cam loose from the herd. Still, Allie and Nick had promised to run interference for me if they could. I was just going to have to make the best of it.

I finished my laces, then sat up and pulled my warmest gloves back on. That made my hands feel a little less like blocks of ice, though it didn't help my face, which had gone numb. Who needs Botox when you have an Arctic air mass?

Nick already had his skates on. He was swinging his arms back and forth, trying to stay warm as he waited for the rest of us to finish getting ready. "Hey Bruce," he said, "where's your man Cam? Thought he said he'd be here."

Good question. I wanted to check my watch, but it was hidden under three or four layers of clothing.

Bruce was sitting on a bench playing snowplow with his skate blades in a handy drift. "Yeah, he'll be along. Probably late though. That new girlfriend of his takes forever getting ready to go out." He stood up and sidled over to me. Even with a frozen face, he could still leer. Amazing. "Guess she's not the natural woman type like you, eh, Lexi?"

Before I could answer, I heard a car door slam. I glanced over toward the parking lot, my heart jumping. But it was only Allie. She'd been changing into a borrowed pair of Nick's extra-warm wool socks in his car.

But behind her, I finally saw a familiar

car pulling into the lot. "Cam's here," I hissed at Nick.

Bruce spotted the car at the same time. "Finally. Here they are."

He headed over to greet the newcomers. The rest of us drifted along after him, walking awkwardly across the snowy lawn in our skates and guards.

Cam climbed out of the car first and waved. Then he hurried around to the other side to let Jaylene out.

"What, is she incapable of opening a car door for herself?" I muttered to Allie.

She shot me a sympathetic glance. "Be fair," she said. "You can't blame Jaylene because Cam's a gentleman."

"Oh yeah? Just watch me." I scowled as Cam bent over the passenger side door.

A moment later Jaylene emerged. My frozen eyeballs bulged as I got a look at her. Sure, technically what she was wearing could be considered appropriate for skating. But only if the skating in question was in the Ice Capades. She was dressed in a snug Irish wool sweater, a flippy little lavender miniskirt, and shiny white tights. To top it off, a navy-and-white striped scarf was looped jauntily around her neck. At least she was wearing a hat today. It matched the scarf perfectly.

"Oh mah gosh, y'all!" she called out to us, laughing in little bursts that were visible in the cold air. "Ah guess Ah may be kind of underdressed fer this shindig."

Cam swung his battered old hockey skates by their laces, looking sheepish. "She thought we were going to an indoor rink," he explained. "I guess I should have been more specific when I told her about this—she's still not used to, you know, being in the north."

Jaylene waved her hands, which were as usual encased in cute but awfully thin-looking white mittens. "No, Ah'll be fine," she insisted. "Of course, Ah might need a little help to stay warm, if ya'll know what Ah mean!" She grabbed Cam and snuggled up against him.

"Aw, young love," one of the music class gigglers called out. "Aren't they adorable?"

"Sweet," Bruce agreed. "Yo Jaylene, how is it you can look freezing cold and smokin' hot at the same time?"

Jaylene giggled, swinging her hips a little so her skirt danced. "Oh, Bruce. You're such a nut!"

I gritted my chattering teeth. The worst part was, Bruce's obnoxious comment was true. The outfit Jaylene was wearing was totally inappropriate for the occasion. But she *did* look ridiculously hot.

Still, I figured in that get-up Jaylene wouldn't last long on the ice. I was glad I'd brought plenty of hot chocolate—it was already bubbling away in Mom's portable party beverage dispenser, which was plugged in in one of the little cement picnic shelters nearby. With any luck, Jaylene would give up on skating within minutes and camp out in there to stay warm. All I had to do was distract Cam enough to keep him from following her in there. If it was awkward watching her cling to him now, I didn't want to think about catching a glimpse of them making out or something.

"Come on, everybody," I called out with forced cheer. "Why are we all standing around here? We'll be a lot warmer once we get moving."

"She's right." Nick waved an arm toward the lake. "Let's skate!"

I felt a little better once I was out on the ice. My parents and aunt and uncle started taking me and Nick skating as soon as we were old enough to stand up on our own, and I still loved it. The ice was solid in the inlet, though I knew it was probably still a little iffy farther out in the deeper parts of the lake. I forgot about everything else for the moment as I swooped forward, doing some big loopy circles and figure eights to work out the kinks.

The rest of us had left Cam and Jaylene putting on their skates. After a few minutes, I glanced over to see how they were doing. I was just in time to see Cam lead a wobbly-looking Jaylene down the slight incline and onto the ice.

Allie swooped over to me, executing a neat T-stop. "Think she knows how to skate?"

"Nick asked Cam about that," I replied, not taking my eyes off the pair. "Apparently she's skated a few times, but she's not very good."

We watched as she pushed off, clinging to one of Cam's hands with both of hers. Two or three strokes in, her left skate skidded out from under her, quickly followed by the other. She would have fallen if Cam hadn't been holding onto her. Once he'd set her on her feet again, she collapsed against him, laughing.

"Oh mah gosh!" her giddy voice floated across the lake. "This is even harder than Ah remember!"

But before long she was upright and sliding along with tiny, choppy, tentative strokes like a little kid. Cam practically had to skate backward to stay with her at that (lack of) speed.

Nick glided over to Allie and me, both hands tucked into his jeans pockets. "Looks like Cam's doing some babysitting," he said in a low voice. "It's going to be hard to peel her off of him."

"Tell me about it," I said. "But you guys promised to do what you could, right?"

Allie nodded. "Come on, Nick. You taught beginner lessons that one winter, right? Why don't we go offer your expertise to poor Jaylene?"

My friends are brilliant. Within minutes, they'd commandeered Jaylene, pushing Cam out to watch as they took Jaylene by each arm and taught her some basics. I waited until Jaylene looked good and distracted, then skated over to Cam.

"Hey," I greeted him, doing a little backward circle on the ice in front of him. "Having fun?"

"Sure." He smiled at me. "It's kind of cold, but hey, what's a little frostbite when it comes to a friend's birthday?"

"Huh? Oh, right." I'd almost forgotten that we were all supposed to be there for Nick. "So anyway, it looks like Jaylene is learning fast now that those two have ahold of her."

"Yeah. I just hope she doesn't get too chilled." He looked worried. "I really should have warned her we'd be skating outside."

Personally, I thought he was being way too hard on himself. What kind of Southern-fried nutjob expects indoor skating in December in a town located on the shore of a huge frozen lake? But I didn't bother to point that out.

"I'm sure she'll be fine," I said. "Once you start moving around out here, it's not so bad. Speaking of which, want to take a spin around the inlet while she's having her lesson? You know, for old time's sake."

"Sure, I guess." Cam shot another glance at Jaylene, who had just slipped again and was clinging to Nick's waist while Allie tried to haul her back to her feet without skidding out herself. I wasn't sure Cam had even caught the "for old time's sake" bit in my invitation.

"Let's go, then," I said as cheerfully as I could. "Last one to the swimming platform's a rotten egg!"

In summer, the skating inlet became the swimming inlet. There was an ancient, half-rotted wooden platform that had been out there since sometime before my parents were born. It was pretty much unofficially condemned at this point—kids only ever climbed on it as a dare. But it still floated out there, making a handy end point for racing whether the water was frozen or not.

I took off toward it, pushing out faster and faster to work up speed. After a moment I glanced back over my shoulder. Cam was a few yards back. I could tell he wasn't going anywhere near full-out—he always let me win, no matter how many times I scolded him about it, saying it was sexist.

I skidded to a stop once I reached the platform, spinning around and waiting for him to catch up. When he got there he was smiling, his cheeks showing the two rosy little spots he always got when he exerted himself.

"You win, as usual," he said. "I should know better than to even try."

That sort of comment used to annoy me

a little. After all, it wasn't as if I needed him to let me beat him at speed skating. It was one thing for my dad to do that when I was five, but Cam was supposed to be my boyfriend—my equal.

Only he wasn't my boyfriend anymore, and somehow that made it seem more sweet than annoying. That Nostalgia Footnote thing was obviously working on *me*.

"Winner and still champion," I said lightly. Suddenly remembering one of Allie's older theories—the Touchy-Feely Theory—I reached over and punched him lightly on the arm. "How about a rematch? Shore and back?"

"Maybe later." His gaze had wandered back across the ice toward where Nick and Allie were still guiding their pupil along. "I should probably go back and check on Jaylene."

My heart sank. So much for trusting in those theories.

"Okay," I said, feeling a little desperate. "But wait, first you've got to see my new move. Double axel."

"Really?" He turned back to me, looking impressed. "I had no idea you'd been practicing that, Lexi."

The truth was, I hadn't. I'd only seen skaters do it on TV. But what did I have to lose? I could do a single axel in my sleep. If I pulled off a double on my first try, yay me. If not and I wiped out, Cam would have to rush to my aid. Right? With any luck I'd be injured and he'd be stuck nursing me while the others rushed to call 911. . . .

I was so lost in that wacked-out little fantasy that it took me a moment to notice that he was sort of drifting back in the direction of the others. It was now or never.

"Here I go!" I sang out, not stopping to think about what I was about to attempt. At least if I broke both my arms and legs, my college applications were already finished.

I pushed off, picking up speed quickly, aiming toward a broad patch of smooth ice toward the north end of the inlet. Faster. Faster. I raised one leg and got into position. My heart pounded as the sane part of my brain screamed at me to stop. The uninhabited wooded shoreline over there was getting closer, and I had to go soon or else give up and turn back.

Thinking of Cam, I went. I might have

closed my eyes for a second. Then I pushed off—and spun. Once around. Twice. A second later I felt the blade of my landing skate connect cleanly with the ice. I'd done it!

"Whoa!" I heard Bruce call out from over near the shore. "Did you guys see that? That was amazing, Lexi!"

But I didn't care what *he* thought of it. I glanced back toward Cam. He was smiling. But then his expression switched over to one of alarm.

"Lexi, look out!" he called. "You're heading straight for the—"

SPLASH!

The ice collapsed beneath me. *"Aaaah!"* I screeched as I sank into freezing-cold water up almost to my thighs.

It was only then that I recognized my mistake. The spring. We'd all had it pounded into us since we were kids: *Don't skate too close to the spring.* The water there bubbled up from underground, constantly moving, and therefore it was the only part of the inlet that never fully froze, even in the coldest depths of February.

And what had I done? I'd skated right into it. Brilliant. It was a good thing old Mrs. Simpson hadn't been there to witness my stupidity, or that Simpson Scholarship would have been Andrew's for sure.

Luckily the water isn't very deep that close to shore. By the time my friends reached me, I had clambered my way onto dry—well, make that *snowy*—land with soaked legs, chattering teeth, and bruised ego.

"Lexi, what were you thinking?" Allie exclaimed. "You know better than to get so close to the spring!"

Jaylene arrived only a moment after the others, so her lessons must have been working. "What happened?" she cried. "Oh mah gosh—skating outside is so *dangerous*!"

The cold was seeping into my bones, giving me an overall feeling of numb pessimism. I expected Cam to rush over and give Jaylene a detailed topographical lecture on Lake Claus. But instead he shrugged off his ski jacket and draped it around me.

"Come on," he said. "We've got to get you dried off."

Nick reached into his pocket and pulled out his keys. "Stick her in my car," he said, tossing the keys to Cam. "It has the best heater. Also, I think there's a pair of sweats in the back."

Cam caught the keys and put an arm around my shoulders. "Come on, Lexi."

My teeth were still chattering, which was probably a good thing. Otherwise I probably would have been grinning like a fool. I shot Allie a quick, triumphant look.

Who needs nostalgia theories when good ol' hypothermia works even faster? I thought as I allowed Cam to pull me back onto the ice and across the lake in the direction of the inlet park.

Soon I was huddled in the passenger seat of Nick's car, dressed in Nick's faded old sweatpants, my bare feet propped up on the dashboard to get them closer to the heat vent. Cam's jacket was still around me; it smelled faintly of his aftershave.

Meanwhile Cam himself was in the driver's seat. He fiddled with the heat blowers, pointing all of them in my direction.

"Feeling okay?" he asked. "Can you wriggle your toes? Do you think you have frostbite?"

"I'm okay." I wriggled my toes to show him. "I was only in the water for a few seconds."

"Good." He glanced out the car window.

"So," I blurted out, guessing that he was

thinking about heading back out there to where Jaylene was surely waiting for him, "this reminds me of our very first date."

"Huh?" He blinked at me. "What do you mean?"

I laughed. "Um, not the frostbite and stuff," I said. "I mean the skating. Remember? Our first date, the two of us out there on the lake . . ."

He shook his head, his brow furrowing slightly. "Skating wasn't our first date, Lexi," he said, suddenly sounding kind of sad. "It was our second. Our first date was the Christmas movie at the North Pole."

Oops. Now that he mentioned it . . .

"Oh, right," I said. "Sorry. Um, must be frostbite of the brain."

His smile looked wistful. "You know, I'm starting to think maybe you were right all along. I wasn't sure this—this breakup was the best thing. But it could be that we're better off as friends, you know? Even if I didn't want to accept it at first . . ."

No! My brain stalled out, and I could almost feel Nick and Allie perched on my shoulders, like the little angel and devil figures you see in sitcoms and comic strips sometimes. Only they were both on the same shoulder, poking me in the head and yelling, "Tell him the truth! Tell him the truth!"

And at that moment, I wondered if maybe they were right. I'd made a big mistake playing games with our relationship in the first place. Was it time for the games to stop?

"Listen, Cam . . . ," I began.

Just then there was a knock on the driver's side window. A moment later the door opened and Jaylene stuck her cheerful face into the warm car.

"Ya'll okay in here?" she asked brightly. "Lexi, Ah hope you didn't freeze your little toesies off, fallin' in that freezin' cold water like that!"

I forced a smile. "No, my toesies are all still attached."

Cam was already climbing out of the car. "I think you'll be okay, Lex," he told me as Jaylene latched onto his arm like a five-foot blond leech. "You might want to stay in the heat for a while, though. Maybe drink some hot cocoa to help warm up."

"Thanks, doc," I said, that fake smile still plastered on my face.

But as soon as they were out of sight, I closed my eyes and blew out a frustrated sigh. So close and yet so far . . .

Ten

"The More Than Friends Theory," Allie said.

"What?" Nick and I both looked up from our burgers.

The three of us were sitting in one of the deep, private window booths at the Elf Street Diner, eating dinner and talking over that afternoon's disastrous skating party. A reggae version of "God Rest Ye Merry Gentlemen" was rolling softly out of the speaker over our table, doing a pretty good job of drowning out the conversations of the other customers and the rattles and clinks of the cooks and waitresses at work.

"It's just what it sounds like." Allie reached for a french fry from the communal plate in the center of our table. "We all agree that what's needed here is to remind Cam of what he's missing by being just friends, right?"

"Sure, I guess," I replied. Nick shrugged.

"Okay," Allie went on. "Then the More Than Friends Theory states that you have to *show* him what he's missing by being 'just friends.' You know, by being sexy. Seducing him. That kind of thing."

Nick laughed. "Yeah, right," he said sarcastically, looking me up and down. "That's going to happen."

"Shut up." I had to admit I wasn't exactly looking the part of seductress at the moment, dressed as I was in a pair of plaid flannel pants and one of my dad's shabby old University of Wisconsin sweatshirts. But that wasn't really the point. "He's kind of right, though, Allie. That doesn't exactly sound like me. Or like Cam, for that matter."

Allie dipped her fry in ketchup. "That's what you said about him liking Jaylene. Anyway, desperate times call for desperate measures. How many dates are they up to now, anyway?"

"Five," I said before I could stop myself. "Um, but who's counting? Anyway, I'm still not convinced on this Dozen Dates thing in the first place, or— What?" I interrupted myself as Allie's eyes widened.

"Five? But that means the next date is number six."

"And people say *I'm* good at math," I teased.

She shook her head. "No, listen, Lexi. I've been working some more on the Dozen Dates Theory. According to the Halfway Point Addendum, your task gets harder from date six on. Um, you know, exponentially."

"Expressing your theories in mathematical terms now, are you?" I commented with a laugh, reaching for the salt. "I guess it's always important to know your audience. Did you learn that from Oprah?"

Nick chortled, but Allie didn't even crack a smile. "I'm serious, Lexi. You need to do something."

I stopped laughing. "Do you think I don't know that? It's killing me to think that I might have messed things up with Cam for good. You know that."

"I know." Her expression softened. "But see, that's exactly why you need to be willing to try whatever it takes to get him back. And we all know that guys think mostly with their hormones." Ignoring Nick's snort, she went on, "So our best bet is to let him see you in some supersexy outfit that will remind him of just how attracted he is to you."

"What, do you want me to wear some lacy little number from Victoria's Secret to school on Monday? Then again, why be subtle? Maybe I should just show up on his doorstep stark naked."

"You're right, showing up at his house is probably too obvious." She chose to ignore the rest of my suggestion, which was just as well. In her current state, she might actually think I was serious. "No, you might have to work it right in front of Jaylene on this one. In fact, maybe that's better anyway. Let him see exactly what he's given up to be with her." She nodded, looking pleased with herself. "Okay, so that means we have to find out when and where their next date is."

Nick grabbed another fry. "I already know," he said. "Cam was talking about it at the lake today. They're going bowling tomorrow night."

"Hmm, bowling. That doesn't sound

very sexy." Allie tapped one finger on her chin. I could almost see the little gears in her brain turning. "But never mind—I'm sure we can still come up with an outfit that will turn his head. Is Cam more of a leg man or a boob man?" When I shrugged, she turned to my cousin. "Nick?"

He looked a bit startled. "How should I know?"

"Isn't that what you guys talk about? You know, in the locker room and stuff?"

He rolled his eyes. "If we do, I'm not about to start discussing it with the two of you." Setting down his half-finished burger, he wiped his hands on a napkin and stood up. "In fact, all this talk of boob men and sexy outfits for my cousin makes me think it's a good time for a nice long game of pinball. See you."

He scooted off toward the line of arcade games along the side wall. "See that, Allie?" I reached across the table, peeled the pickle off Nick's burger, and popped it into my mouth. "You made him lose his appetite. That's not easy. Congratulations."

"Now that he's gone, let's get down to business." Allie shoved her plate away and leaned forward. "What are you going to wear to the bowling alley tomorrow night? How about your purple cami? I'm working on a theory about how guys really notice the color purple."

"Um, I don't think so. In case it's slipped your mind, it's December. If I show up in something like that, Cam won't think I'm sexy; he'll think I've gone insane." I wiped my pickley fingers on my napkin. "No, I'm thinking maybe I'll wear my green V-neck sweater. Nick always compliments me on that one. Says it brings out the gold in my eyes."

She looked disappointed. "Okay, I guess that'll have to do. So let's talk strategy. Maybe you can, like, lure him off by himself somewhere and then pretend you have a cramp in your leg, and ask him to rub it for you."

"Are you kidding?" I laughed. "I'm not going to do that."

"But the Dozen Dates Theory . . . ," she began urgently.

I shook my head. "I know, I know. There isn't much time. I get that. But even so, I think I just need to keep things simple. Cam isn't the type of guy to fall for anything too obvious. And plotting and scheming is what got me into this mess to begin with."

"That's true," Allie agreed, reaching for her iced tea. "Okay. But you're not just going to, like, stand there, right? Let's talk about the little things you can do to catch his attention."

"Like what?"

"Don't look so suspicious," she said. "I just mean stuff like smiling at him. Touching him on the arm whenever you get the chance. That sort of thing."

I felt as if I should be taking notes. It hadn't required nearly this much effort to win Cam over in the first place, and I felt kind of foolish having to work so hard at getting him back now. Still, I figured I had to do whatever it took to undo what I'd done.

Walking into the bowling alley all by myself felt weird. For one thing, I'm not much of a bowler. I'd probably only ever been there four or five times total in my life. Plus it's really the kind of place people normally go as part of a big group. To top it off, Allie had twisted my arm until I'd agreed to put on a little extra makeup before I went. I guess that was to make up for the fact that I'd continued to insist on wearing jeans and a sweater rather than the leather bustier and hot pants she probably thought would be much more ideal.

As soon as I got inside, I heard an ear-splitting screech of laughter. Glancing that way, I saw Jaylene dancing around giddily in her adorable lemon yellow minidress, giggling loudly as the gutterball she'd just thrown ambled its way down the lane. Cam was watching her from the scorekeeper's seat, with his long legs splayed out to one side and his arm draped casually over the seat back. But he spotted me a second later and sat up straight.

"Lexi?" he called out, sounding surprised. No wonder. As I mentioned, I'm not exactly the bowling queen of Claus Lake.

Jaylene looked over too. "It *is* Lexi!" she cried, waving at me. "C'mon over here, Lexi!"

I obeyed, ducking around the molded orange plastic chairs to enter their seating area. "What a surprise," I said. "So you guys are doing a little bowling tonight, huh?"

"Yeah." Cam stood up, looking kind of awkward. "Um, what are you doing here?"

I had my cover story ready, of course. "Oh, I was supposed to meet Nick here on my way home from shopping. He was in the mood for bowling—you know how he gets ideas in his head sometimes."

Cam chuckled. "Uh-huh." He glanced at Jaylene. "If Nick decides he wants to do something, it's easier just to go along with it. Otherwise he'll hound you until you give in."

"Right." I smiled weakly, trying not to calculate exactly how many lies I'd told Cam by now. "But anyway, he just called my cell to say he has a flat tire and can't make it after all. So I ducked inside for a few minutes to warm up before I head home."

"Oh, y'all don't have to go home," Jaylene said brightly. "Why don't you join us? It'll be fun!"

On the one hand I was relieved, since getting invited to hang with them was the point of the whole plan. On the other hand, couldn't Jaylene at least seem a *teensy* bit threatened at having Cam's ex crash their date?

"Well . . ." I pretended to think it over for a second. "Sure, I guess that would be fun. Thanks."

"Hey, check it out—Sexy Lexi's here!"

I spun around. "Bruce?" I blurted out in surprise. He was walking toward us from the direction of the snack bar, the usual cocky grin on his face and a plastic tray of nachos and sodas in his hands.

"That's right," Jaylene told him. "Lexi's going to join us."

"Cool." Bruce dumped the food on the scoring table and brushed off his hands on his pants. "Now I won't be a third wheel anymore. Or at least I'll have a cute fourth wheel keeping me company." He stepped closer and slung one arm around my shoulders, giving me a squeeze.

I somehow managed *not* to punch him in the head in return. This was definitely not part of the plan. How was I supposed to work on Cam with Bruce drooling all over me?

Still, it seemed too late to abort the mission now. So I trooped over to trade in my Skechers for a pair of smelly red, white, and blue bowling nerd shoes. And for the next hour, I pretended to have a good time while simultaneously fending off Bruce's wandering hands and watching Jaylene giggle and bounce and kiss Cam on the forehead every three seconds and generally be exactly the kind of girl that I wasn't. And yet Cam didn't seem to mind, though I did catch him shooting me weird looks every so often, as if wondering what I was doing there. No wonder. I was wondering that myself.

Still, I did my best to keep hope alive. I kept waiting for that magic moment when Jaylene and Bruce would both wander off to the restroom or the snack bar at the same time, leaving me alone to wow Cam with my irresistible charm and wit.

Finally, after one too many gutter balls, Bruce decided his bowling shoes were at fault and stomped off to the counter get a different pair. At the same time, Jaylene drained her soda cup.

"Think Ah'll get another pop," she said.

Cam immediately stood up. "I'll go," he offered.

But she waved him off. "It's okay, sweetie," she said. "Ah can go mahself. Be right back!"

She strolled off toward the snack bar. Cam glanced at me. He looked kind of uncomfortable. I knew how he felt. Being together used to be so easy, so natural. Now it was as if just hanging out with

Cam had turned into the world's hardest school assignment, a test I desperately needed to pass but hadn't studied for nearly enough.

"Um . . . I think it's your turn, Lexi," he said.

Setting down my soda cup, I stood up and took a step toward the little ball-return thingy. The ball I'd been using all evening, a blue one with green swirls, was right at the front of the line. One of the extras, on the other hand, was sitting at the other end of the machine. It was a little smaller than mine, with gold speckles on a black background. I stared at it, realizing that if I went to grab it instead of the other one, it would force me to lean over Cam's legs, which were sprawled out into the path as usual. My leg might brush against his. Or my hand might rest briefly on his knee to balance myself as I picked up the heavy ball. It was even possible that my thick, curly hair—the hair he'd always loved and complimented—would fall into his face. It would be easy to make it all happen. All I would have to do is reach for that other ball, claim that my old one was cramping my game, like Bruce with his shoes. Or that the old one was pinching my fingers. Or any other number of excuses. It would be so easy. . . .

I knew what Allie would have advised. I knew what someone like Jaylene would have done as instinctively as she drew in a breath one second and blew it out the next.

Somehow, though, I just couldn't do it. After all the trickery I'd pulled, the lies I'd told, it just seemed like one step too far somehow. Call me stupid—I suspected even in that moment that my friends certainly would. But I just grabbed my regular ball and stepped up to the lane. My fingers were shaking a little as I shoved them into the holes.

"Straight and steady, Lexi." Cam leaned forward to watch me. "Don't think about it—just do it."

That made me smile. It was just so . . . Cam.

I glanced at him over my shoulder. "Remember who you're talking to here," I joked. "Since when does it ever work to tell me not to think?"

He grinned. "Good point. Okay, so pretend it's a trig problem or something then, and just throw the ball straight!"

I laughed and threw the ball. It wobbled halfway down the lane, then rolled into the gutter.

"Rats! So much for that trig scholarship to MIT," I said.

Cam laughed. I did too. And just like that, the awkwardness between us dissipated. For that moment, it was as if nothing had changed.

Unfortunately, the moment only lasted, well, a moment. Then Bruce came stomping back, a satisfied look on his face and a pair of identical-looking bowling shoes on his feet.

"You should have seen the soles of those things," he announced, blasting into the seating area and grabbing for his ball. "No wonder I couldn't anchor my throws! You guys had better look out now. . . ."

My brief-lived moment of contentment flickered out. What had I been thinking? I'd just squandered my chance to rekindle things with Cam on stupid trigonometry jokes and actual, you know, *bowling*. It wouldn't have taken some stupid flirty move like switching balls to make things happen. All I'd needed to do was talk to him. Remind him of what we'd had together. Maybe tell him I missed him.

Promising myself I wouldn't waste a second chance, I settled in to wait for it. But it never happened. Instead I eventually found myself alone in the bowling pod with Bruce while Cam was getting more drinks and Jaylene was powdering her nose.

It was Bruce's turn to bowl, but he stayed planted on the seat next to me. "So Lexi," he began. "I meant to ask you at the lake yesterday, but I forgot when you decided to turn it into a swimming party." He grinned and waggled his thin, pale eyebrows up and down. "How about we go out again sometime? The Ball's coming up in a just couple weeks if you don't have a date yet. . . ."

"Oh. Um . . ." I shot a look at Cam to make sure he was out of hearing range. "I don't know. I was sort of planning to just go with Nick and Allie. You know, Nick's still kind of bummed about Rachel, and, well, you know."

"Aw, c'mon, beautiful." He reached over and stroked my cheek. As if *that* was going to be a selling point, especially since his fingers reeked of Cheez Whiz and jalapeño peppers. "Just this once, I want to have a date lined up for the Ball before the Cam man does."

"You mean Cam isn't going with Jaylene?" I tried to keep my voice casual, though it wasn't easy.

Bruce shrugged. "I dunno. Probably," he said. "But as far as I know, he hasn't asked her yet. Maybe he wants to keep his options open. I mean, the poor dude was tied down for a loooong time, you know." Suddenly realizing what he'd just said, he grinned apologetically. "Hey, you know what I mean. No offense or whatever."

That made me feel much less uncomfortable about turning him down. "Now that you mention it, I feel the same way. So that's definitely a thanks but no thanks on the Ball. No offense or whatever."

Cam and Jaylene both returned at that moment. "So whose turn is it?" Jaylene chirped. "Lexi? Aren't you up next?"

I stood up and checked my watch. "Actually, I think I'd better head out," I said. "It's been fun, but it *is* a school night, and I have a physics test tomorrow."

"Aw, you sure?" Jaylene actually looked disappointed. I wasn't sure whether to be flattered or insulted.

"We were only going to bowl one more frame anyway," Cam put in.

"Sorry." I was already reaching for my coat. "You guys will just have to finish without me."

Eleven

"So what kind of costume do you want to get?" I asked Allie as we stepped into the mall the next day after school.

The place was busy for a weekday. Cheery holiday tunes poured out of every storefront, competing with each other and with the equally cheery holiday music playing constantly in the concourse. Hurried-looking shoppers went dashing from store to store or lined up at the coffee place to fuel up for more shopping.

Allie smiled at a little kid racing past us toward the Santa pavilion in the fountain court. "Not sure," she said. "Just something Christmassy and cute, I guess."

I realized she hadn't been talking much

lately about her goal to land herself a boyfriend before the Ball, though now that I thought about it, I wondered if it was a lingering hope that she'd be going as part of a couple that had made her wait so late to get herself a costume. But I kept quiet about that. Allie was a pretty chipper person in general, but the one topic that could get her bleak and gloomy like no other was her love life—or lack thereof. I didn't want to bring her down by making her focus on her single status.

Instead I returned to our previous topic of conversation. *My* love life. Or lack thereof.

"So anyway," I said as we strolled down the bustling mall concourse toward the costume shop, "the one interesting thing that came out of that disaster of a 'double date' at the bowling alley was this: Bruce mentioned that Cam hasn't asked Jaylene to the Ball yet."

"Really?" Allie glanced over, brows lifted in surprise. "That *is* interesting. I wonder if he's afraid she'll say no if he asks her too soon. I came up with a theory about that once—it's called the Delayed Date Theory. It helps explain why guys are so lame about stuff like asking girls to the prom before the last possible second."

We turned the corner and immediately had to dodge an empty baby stroller being pushed kamikaze-style down the mall by a wild-eyed toddler. Barely escaping with our kneecaps intact, we hurried down the concourse and ducked into the costume shop. The song selection there was a jazzy instrumental version of "Deck the Halls." Or "Deck the Malls," as Cam had always jokingly sang it to me whenever we'd heard it under similar circumstances.

"But never mind that," Allie continued. "What we need right now is to get back to the More Than Friends Theory. Just because it didn't work out on the first try doesn't mean you should give up."

"I don't know, Allie." I stepped over to the closest rack and started flipping absentmindedly through the costumes. I'd been pondering the whole Cam situation all day, with only a brief break to focus on and pass my physics test. "I'm starting to wonder if maybe I'm trying too hard."

Allie was pawing through the costumes too. "Wow, the pickings are pretty slim here. I guess most people already have their costumes. Hey, but this one is cute." She grabbed a sparkly white Christmas Angel costume and held it up. "Come on, I want to try it on. You can come with me and explain exactly what the heck you're talking about with the 'trying too hard' stuff."

We headed toward the dressing rooms at the back of the store. "I just wonder if I'm panicking for nothing, that's all," I said as we pushed our way between two racks of Santa suits. "I mean, Cam can't really be happy with someone like Jaylene long-term, can he? What if I just wait it out? After all, if he hasn't even asked her to the Ball yet, maybe he's only with her because he thinks that's what *I* want."

"What?" Allie looked alarmed. "Lexi, no! Think about what you're saying here. I mean, maybe you're right. But he's too special a guy to take that kind of chance. If you let that blond little Southern-fried—"

She let out an audible gulp as we rounded the corner into the dressing-room aisle. For a second I thought she'd stepped on a pin or something.

Then I saw what she'd seen. Or rather *who* she'd seen.

"Well, hi there!" Jaylene exclaimed, her face brightening as she spotted us. She was standing in front of the big full-length mirror on the wall opposite the individual dressing room stalls. "Y'all are just in time to give me your opinion. What do y'all think of this outfit?"

She twirled around in front of the mirror, showing off the costume she had on. It appeared to be meant to represent some kind of elf, though I couldn't imagine any living creature surviving North Pole temperatures with that much flesh showing. The strapless green satin top laced up the front like a corset, hugging her curves and showing an impressive amount of décolletage. The flouncy little skirt—with the emphasis on *little*—was striped like a candy cane, with a hem that appeared to have been dipped in glitter. Jingle bells chimed on the perky hat atop Jaylene's blond curls and the pointy toes of her slippers. Elbow-length satin gloves, a green velvet choker, and green fishnet stockings completed the look.

"They call it the Naughty Elf," she explained with a giggle. "Isn't that adorable? Ah'm just so glad they had mah size."

"Um, it's . . . cute?" Allie seemed to be struggling for the right words. "Doesn't look very warm, though. You know, for December."

Jaylene twirled around and craned her neck to check out the back view. "Oh, Ah'm not worried about that," she said. "Ah'm sure once Ah'm out there dancin' with Cam, Ah'll be plenty warm enough."

"Oh! So Cam asked you to the Ball?" Allie asked, sneaking me a quick look.

Jaylene nodded, making the bell on her hat jingle. "Last night when he dropped me off after our date." She smoothed down her tiny skirt. "He tells me everyone dresses up for this thing, so Ah didn't want to waste any time gettin' started shoppin' for a costume and miss out on all the good ones. Ah bet he'll just love this outfit, don't y'all think so?"

I couldn't quite seem to respond. Seeing Jaylene there in the flesh—*lots* of flesh—in her sexy elf costume had apparently robbed me of the power of speech.

Luckily Allie wasn't similarly afflicted. "Well, since you asked," she said, "I'm not sure that outfit is, um, exactly Cam's cup of tea. He's more the fuzzy reindeer or snowman type of guy. Right, Lexi?"

"Yeah," I blurted out, trying not to stare

at Jaylene's cleavage. "He's kind of, you know, conservative that way."

"Oh, come on, y'all!" Jaylene shimmied in front of the mirror, smiling blissfully as she took in her own reflection. "What self-respectin' man *wouldn't* love a cute lil' costume like this? Ah think Ah'll get it. Thanks a bunch for the input, though, y'all!"

She jingled off back to her dressing room stall. Allie grabbed my arm and yanked me into an empty cubicle nearby.

"That was close!" she hissed into my ear. "Do you think she heard us talking about her when we were coming in?"

"Didn't seem like it. That corset she's wearing probably cut off the blood supply to her ears."

"Shh!" Allie looked alarmed. "Let's not talk until—you know." She tilted her head in the general direction of Jaylene's dressing room stall.

She hung the angel costume on the door and started peeling off her clothes. I slumped on the hard triangular seat in the corner of the stall and waited, staring off into space. I was fine with not talking for a few minutes. Maybe that would give me time to figure out whether I'd really known Cam as well as I thought I did.

Allie was adjusting the halo on her outfit when a tap came on our door. "See y'all later!" Jaylene called in to us.

"Bye," Allie and I called back.

We waited until we were pretty sure she was out of earshot. Then I let out a long breath of frustration. "Listen, Allie," I said. "Do you think I wasn't trying hard enough with Cam?"

"Make up your mind—are you trying too hard, or not hard enough? Anyway, what do you mean?" Allie tugged at the hem of her white skirt. "Like, last night at the bowling alley? I already told you, I—"

"No, not that." I sat up straight and stared at her. "I'm just starting to wonder if Cam was actually as happy in our relationship as I always assumed. Is he really just a conservative, fuzzy-reindeer-costume kind of guy? Or would he maybe have appreciated a little more excitement, a little more naughty elf or whatever, and I wasn't trying hard enough to see that?"

Allie's eyes widened. "Oh, Lexi . . ."

"No, really. We thought he'd never go for someone like"—I glanced cautiously toward our cubicle door—"um, you-know-who. But look at them now! Maybe that's what he likes about her. She keeps him on his toes, gives him something fresh and new and sexy and different. Instead of me, who just sort of took him for granted."

"So what are you saying? You're not giving up, are you?"

"No way. Since when do I back down from a challenge?" I smiled grimly. "No, I'm going to do exactly what you've been telling me to do. Pull out that More Than Friends Theory. Give it a real test. Starting with finding my *own* sexy costume for that Christmas Eve Ball."

Allie looked dubious. "Um, are you sure?" she said. "I mean, I know I've been telling you to do the More Than Friends thing. But I'm not sure a head-to-head sexy competition with Jaylene is, you know, the best way to do it. That naughty elf costume was, well . . . and she has, um, you know . . . I'm just not sure how you're going to top that, okay? Maybe it's better if you stick to being yourself."

"What, you mean dress up as a test tube or something?" I grinned to let her know I wasn't insulted. "Anyway, that angel costume looks great on you. So get it off and come out and help me find one for myself."

Despite her doubts, Allie loyally helped me dig through the racks of Christmas costumes. Unfortunately, we didn't have much luck. All that was left in my size were frumpy Mrs. Claus dresses and a snowman costume that would have made me look like the Michelin Man.

Biting my lip, I glanced toward the clearance rack at the back of the store. That was where the leftover Halloween stuff hung, dusty and forgotten amidst all the Yuletide frenzy.

"Come on," I said grimly, heading that way. "Let's see if there's anything we can use over there."

Allie trailed after me. "Maybe you could go as a vampire and try to scare Jaylene back to Georgia," she joked halfheartedly as I dug into the costumes.

"Hey, look at this." I pulled out a shimmering pair of emerald green see-through harem pants. I held them up against my long legs, casting a critical eye downward. "Looks like they'll fit."

"What is that, a genie outfit?" Allie

asked. "That doesn't have anything to do with Christmas."

"And here I thought you were supposed to be the creative one," I said. "All we need are the right accessories. . . ."

A few minutes later I was in the dressing room, twirling around in our creation. In addition to the translucent green harem pants, which billowed gauzily around my legs and allowed free view of my (thankfully clean and hole-free) white panties, I was wearing a green vest with red and white trim that we'd taken from a boy's-sized Santa's-helper outfit. It ended several inches above the waistband of the harem pants and didn't quite close across my chest, so I was also wearing a wide candy-cane-striped headband as a makeshift tube top underneath. Oh, and a festive Santa hat just to top it all off. At first I felt a little queasy at the thought of going out in public with so much of me exposed, but I reminded myself it really wasn't any different from walking around the community swim club in a bikini.

"Ta-da," I announced, twisting around to check out the back. "We can call it a Christmas Genie."

"More like a Rated-Xmas Genie," Allie commented wryly. "Or better yet, a Triple-Xmas Genie."

"I don't care what you call it." I stared at my reflection, trying to imagine what Cam's reaction would be when he saw me in it on Christmas Eve. Jaylene wasn't the only one who could make his life fresh and exciting. "All I care about is that it works."

Twelve

The sales clerk at the costume shop seemed a little dubious as she rang up the various parts of my costume. But I didn't care. This was going to work—it had to.

"So what's your plan?" Allie asked as we headed back out into the mall concourse with our shopping bags. "Are you just going to show up in that outfit at the Ball and see what happens?"

"Yeah, I guess so." I bit my lip, realizing I hadn't really thought this through. That wasn't like me. "Um, maybe when I get there I can go over and ask Cam to dance, and then . . . Oh, who am I kidding?" I cried, tossing my bag onto a nearby bench and then flopping down next to it.

"This is never going to work. You're right—I can't compete with Jaylene when it comes to this sort of thing. She's all cute and flirty and sexy without even trying, and that's so not my thing. I can't even imagine going out in public wearing this trashy thing!" I poked at the bag containing the costume.

Allie sat down and patted me on the knee. "Don't freak out, Lexi. It'll be okay."

"How can you say that?" I glared at her. "You're the one telling me I only have a dozen dates and then Cam is gone forever. Maybe all this scheming and planning is just a big stupid waste of time. Maybe I should just call him up right here and now and come clean about the whole mess—throw myself on his mercy and beg him to take me back."

I reached into my purse and grabbed my cell phone. It would be so easy to hit that speed dial button. . . .

Allie looked excited. "Oh, that's a fantastic idea!" she exclaimed. "Do it, Lexi. Call him. Tell him the truth. He'll forgive you—I know he will. It's just like my Candid Couple Theory. Even when times are difficult or someone has messed up, being honest is usually the best way to fix your relationship, even if it sometimes makes things seem even worse for a while."

That brought me back to earth with a thud. I stared at my phone.

"Yeah," I said slowly. "Being honest usually fixes things. Except when it makes things even worse *permanently* because the trust is gone. Am I really willing to take the chance of losing Cam forever once he hears how crazy and deceitful I've been about all this? He'll never be able to look at me the same way again."

"But this is you and Cam we're talking about," Allie said. "Of course he'll forgive and forget. That's the way he is."

"How do you know that? What if he doesn't?" I shoved the phone back into my purse. "Sorry, but I can't take the chance. If he decided never to talk to me again . . ." I dropped my head into my hands, feeling self-pity envelop me like a thick, stifling cloak.

"It's okay, Lexi." Allie's moment of hope and glee had passed, and now she just sounded kind of tired. "We all know how you are. You trust your head more than your heart. I'm sure Cam realizes that too."

I barely heard her. "All this time, I just

wanted to save both of us from a little pain and suffering by being practical," I moaned. "But now it seems like I just made things worse on both of us." I paused and frowned. "Well, worse on myself, anyway. Cam doesn't exactly seem to be suffering now that he's with Miss Naughty Elf."

Allie sighed and stood up. "Come on, let's hit the food court. I suddenly feel the need for some serious caffeine."

By the time I got to school the next morning, I had formulated a new plan. I found Cam at his locker. Fortunately he was alone, with Jaylene nowhere in sight.

"Hi, Cam," I greeted him in what I hoped was a normal tone of voice. "Listen, I was just organizing my room over the weekend and I realized I still have a bunch of your CDs and stuff. Do you want to stop by this afternoon and pick them up?"

Cam blinked. "Oh," he said, sounding kind of subdued. "Um, sure. I guess I could do that."

"Great." I smiled, relieved that the pieces were falling into place so easily. "Why don't you stop by around four? I'll be ready for you."

"Okay."

As I hurried away, my heart was pounding at the thought of what I was planning to do. Could I actually pull this off?

Well, one thing's for sure, I thought as I headed down the hall toward my homeroom. *When Cam stops by this afternoon, he definitely isn't going to find the same old boring Lexi who always took him for granted!*

I tucked the phone between my ear and shoulder, leaving both hands free to fiddle with the waistband of my harem pants. I rolled it down carefully, exposing even more of my bare belly.

"So I decided to ditch the vest," I told Allie, who was on the other end of the line. "I mean, why be subtle here, right?"

"If you say so. I just hope you don't give Cam a heart attack."

Giving one last tug at the pants, I then reached up and carefully tweaked my headband/tube top to allow for maximum exposure. Then I took the phone in my hand and switched ears. "Oh, and I'm wearing a thong under the genie pants. Cam always said I have a cute butt." I giggled, trying to keep my nerves under control.

"Anyway, Allie, you should see this outfit. If you thought it was triple-X before . . ."

I surveyed myself in the full-length mirror on the back of my bedroom door. It was a good thing both my parents were out for the afternoon. There was no way they'd let me leave my room looking like that, let alone answer the door.

And answering the door was the plan. When Cam arrived to pick up his stuff at four—right on schedule, as he always was—I was going to "accidentally" answer the door in my Triple-Xmas Genie get-up. I would pretend I'd forgotten about our appointment and thought he was Allie coming over to see the costume. Oopsie! Blush, wink, wriggle . . . and as Jaylene herself might say, what man could resist that, y'all?

"There's the doorbell," I told Allie, glancing at the clock as I heard a chime from downstairs. "He's a little early—it figures. I'll call you later and let you know how it went."

I hung up and tossed the phone onto my bed. Then, with one last glance at my reflection and a quick adjustment to my Santa hat, I headed for the stairs, walking carefully in my mom's tallest spike heels.

When I reached the door I paused, closed my eyes briefly, and took a deep breath, doing my best to calm my nerves. Then I opened my eyes and flung open the door.

"Hi," I said brightly. "I—uh—oh."

I froze. And not only because it was about twenty degrees outside and I was practically naked.

No, it was because there were three people standing on my front porch, and none of them was Cam. I stared in horror from my school principal to ninety-plus-year-old Mrs. Simpson in her wool coat and pearls to some gawky twenty-year-old kid holding a camera.

"Er, good afternoon, Miss Michaels," Principal Jamison stammered, his startled gaze wandering briefly downward before snapping up to my face again. "We're, uh, here to surprise you with the news that you've won the Simpson Scholarship this year."

It worked. I was *definitely* surprised.

Thirteen

Actually, to say I was surprised is an understatement. Stunned was more like it. The gawky kid with the camera had looked kind of bored when I'd opened the door. But now his eyes were practically bulging out of his face. He lifted his camera and quickly snapped a few shots. That jolted me back in action.

"Stop that!" I blurted out, ducking behind the door.

"Sorry." He smirked. "Just doing my job. I'm with the *Claus Lake Courier*."

Mrs. Simpson was peering at me through her spectacles. "Perhaps we should come back at another time, my dear," she said in her quavery voice.

"No, wait!" I said, not wanting to give them the chance to change their minds about that scholarship. "Um, wait here a second. Please. I'll be right back."

I swung the door shut behind me and raced for the coat closet, almost tripping over my own feet in those stupid spike heels. Flinging open the closet, I grabbed my dad's oversized camo-print hunting coat. When I shrugged it on, it came down past my knees. Perfect. Wrapping it around me until nothing showed south of my neck, I headed back toward the door.

"Um, okay," I said, stepping out onto the porch and hoping my face wasn't as crimson as it felt. "Sorry about that . . ."

I'm not sure how I survived the interview that followed, though I do vaguely remember promising the young reporter-photographer to e-mail him a picture of me wearing normal clothes. I tried not to think about where those photos he'd taken of me might end up, but made a mental note to stay off the Internet for a few days just for my own sanity.

We were all still there on the porch when Cam's car pulled into the driveway, right on time as always. He looked confused as he climbed out and took in the sight of me in the camo coat and Mom's heels. "Er . . . Lexi?" he said uncertainly, coming closer.

"Hello there, Mr. Kehoe." Principal Jamison seemed a lot more comfortable now that I was no longer dressed like a stripper. He sounded downright jovial as he greeted Cam. "We're just here bringing Lexi some good news. She's this year's recipient of the Simpson Scholarship."

Cam smiled up at me from the bottom of the porch steps, shoving his hands into his coat pockets. "Congratulations, Lexi," he said. "I knew you could do it. Um, and maybe I should come back another time to, you know . . ."

"Thanks, Cam." I could only watch helplessly as he gave me a wave and then turned and hurried back to his car.

"What about Sugarplums?" Nick said, glancing across the street as he emerged from the steamy interior of the local dry cleaner's shop. "I know we just picked up pledge forms there last week, but they always get a ton."

"Good call." Allie stepped around a

slushy puddle on the sidewalk. It had been a sunny and relatively warm day, and some of the snow that had fallen earlier that week had melted, but now the sun was setting, the wind was picking up, and the slush was starting to harden into ice once again. "Plus while we're there, maybe we can stop and have a hot chocolate or something. I'm freezing!"

I switched my backpack over onto my other shoulder. It was getting heavy. The three of us had been assigned to walk around Claus Lake's main business district that afternoon and pick up the pledge forms that people had been leaving at all the shops and restaurants. The Christmas Eve Costume Ball was a charity event, and in addition to buying tickets and contributing at the Ball itself, townspeople could pledge additional money while they shopped or ate at sponsoring businesses throughout the holiday season. And people seemed to be in a giving mood, judging by the number of pledge cards we were collecting. With less than two weeks to go until Christmas Eve, Claus Lake was reaching a fever pitch of festive spirit, as usual.

But I couldn't seem to focus on any of

that. Not this year. Ever since that embarrassing moment on my front porch the other day, I had been fighting a sense of impending doom. It seemed that every time I tried to win Cam back, something got in my way. And even though I'd never put that much stock in Allie's theories before, I couldn't stop thinking about the Dozen Dates Theory. What if it was true?

I was busy pondering that for the fifty-millionth time as we crossed the street to Sugarplums, the town's most popular ice cream and sweets shop. In fact, I was so deep in thought that I bumped into Allie as she came to a sudden stop in the doorway.

"Hey, what's wrong?" I gave her a poke in the back. "Keep moving—my frostbite is getting frostbite out here."

"Um, I was just thinking." Allie turned and pushed me back a step or two. "I'm not really in the mood for hot chocolate after all. Maybe we should go over to the diner instead."

"What's the matter with you? You love hot choc—" I stopped short. I'd just gotten a look past her at the interior of the sweets shop. Cam and Jaylene were seated at one of the tiny round tables for two, their heads close together as they dug into a shared ice cream sundae.

Their backs were to us, so they didn't see us. While we stood there gawking, Jaylene reached up and wiped something off Cam's cheek. He smiled, and she leaned her blond head against his shoulder for a moment before continuing to eat.

Nick grabbed me by the arm. "Come on," he said. "Allie's right. Suddenly the diner looks like a much more appetizing idea."

Soon the three of us were down the block at the Elf Street Diner, sliding into our usual booth, me on one side, Allie and Nick on the other. My mind was still whirling with what we'd just witnessed.

"If I'm counting right and haven't missed anything, that's date number eight they're on right now," I said. "I've been trying to figure it out mathematically. At the rate they've been going, there's a high probability that the Ball will be date number twelve."

"Oh, Lexi." Allie's expression was anxious and sorrowful. "I wish I'd never even told you about that theory. It's making you too crazy."

"Yeah. Since when do you believe in her

nutty theories, anyway?" Nick said. Shooting Allie a glance, he added, "No offense."

The waitress approached at that moment bearing menus. "We don't need those," Nick told her. "We'll just have three hot cocoas and a basket of fries."

She shrugged. "You got it, hon." After quickly scribbling a note on her pad, she bustled off again.

"Anyway," Nick said to me, "no matter what Allie says, there's nothing magical about date number twelve. It's not like Cam's going to turn into a pumpkin or something."

"I know." I ran my hands through my hair, not even caring for once about Bozoing myself up in public. "I know that. Of course I know that. But it's not really the point, is it?"

"What do you mean?" Allie asked.

I stared at her. "Twelve dates, thirteen . . . at some point, that theory of yours is going to be right. They're going to be a real couple, and it'll be too late for me to get him back." I bit my lip. "And then I may spend the rest of my fabulous, exciting, big-city life wondering if I let my one true love get away."

Allie and Nick exchanged a glance. "Look, Lex," Nick said. "There's a really easy solution to all this angst."

"Don't tell me to just talk to him," I warned.

"But you have to!" Allie cried, leaning forward over the table. "Just tell him the truth already. What's the big deal? You've always been honest with the rest of us."

"Yeah," Nick added. "Even when we didn't ask for it. Like when you made me get rid of those ratty old cargo pants I used to wear all the time."

"Or that time back in middle school when you were the only one who told me my new haircut looked terrible and I should get it fixed," Allie put in. "I was kind of hurt at first, but you were sooo right, and I would've been way more embarrassed if I'd walked around like that for weeks without realizing the truth."

"Oh, and then there was the summer after sixth grade when you convinced me to confess to breaking old Mr. Miller's window," Nick said. "Yeah, he was mad at first, but he was so impressed with the way I took care of his lawn to pay him back that he hired me to mow for the next three summers. So you were right to make me 'fess up."

I held up both hands as Allie opened her mouth again. "Okay, enough. I get the picture. Honesty is the best policy, blah blah blah." The waitress was returning with a tray of water glasses by now, so I paused until she'd set one in front of each of us and then hurried off again. "But this is different," I went on, wrapping both hands around the cool, slick surface of my water glass. "I've dug myself in too deep already. If Cam and I *do* get back together, he can never know what a devious psycho I truly am." I stared at them both. "That means you guys can never tell him either. Promise?"

"Whatever you say, Lexi." Allie sighed and tugged at the loose strand of hair that had fallen out of her ponytail.

"Yeah, Scout's honor and all that." Nick lazily crossed his heart with one finger. "But if you're not going to tell him the truth, how exactly *are* you planning to win him back?"

"Good question." I gulped down half my water, then set down the glass and tapped my fingers on the table, thinking hard. "I definitely can't just beg him to give me another chance. Way too random and pathetic, especially after I spent so much time practically shoving him at Jaylene. No, getting back together has to seem like *his* idea."

"Are you kidding me?" Nick shook his head. "That sort of thinking is exactly what got you into this mess in the first place, remember?"

But I barely heard him. What I'd just said had sparked something. Not a real answer, not quite . . . but the feeling that an answer was just around the corner somehow.

"Throwing myself at Cam isn't going to work," I mused aloud. "I had to practically staple Jaylene to his lap to get him to break up with me." For the first time in, oh, about five or six dates, I felt a flicker of real hope and confidence. "After all, I convinced Cam to decide to break up with me when you guys swore it couldn't be done. It can't be impossible to convince him to decide he has to have me back. All I need is the right plan. . . ."

Fourteen

We were halfway through the basket of fries before I finally hit on a promising idea. "It was one of your theories a while back," I told Allie. "Something about being jealous—Jealous Jumping Beans or something?"

"You mean the Jealousy Jump-Start Theory?" she guessed.

"That's the one. It was something about how a guy who's on the fence about asking a girl out is more likely to do it if he thinks another guy is about to swoop in and snag her."

"Yeah, that's basically it." Allie licked some ketchup off her fingers.. "But that theory is really meant for new couples, not your kind of situation. Plus Cam isn't the competitive type like a lot of guys."

Nick nodded. "True. Otherwise he would've decked his buddy Bruce long ago for slobbering all over you every chance he gets."

"That's different," I said. "Cam knew I never had any interest in Bruce. But think about it. It took me seeing him with Jaylene to truly realize what I was losing when we split up. Maybe if he sees me with another guy—a *real* guy, a hot, mysterious guy, not anyone like Bruce or Andrew—he'll have the same kind of epiphany."

"You know, that *almost* makes sense." Allie sounded dubious, but there was a hint of interest in her voice too. "I guess it could work. Maybe. It would definitely be an interesting expansion of that theory."

"Kind of sucks for your decoy boy if it does work, though," Nick put in. "Are you really going to use some poor dude like that, Lex? Get him all hot and bothered over you, dump him like a bad potato, and then go running back to Cam?"

"Of course not!" I retorted.

To be honest, I hadn't gotten that far yet. But now that I thought about it, I realized my cousin was right. I couldn't treat any guy like some lab rat, no matter how important it was to get Cam back. Maybe a little of Cam's niceness had rubbed off on me over the years after all.

"No," I said thoughtfully, reaching for another french fry, "the other guy will have to be in on the plan." I smiled as the perfect guy popped into my head. "Hey! How about your friend Charlie?"

"You mean Charlie Welles from baseball camp?" Nick asked.

"Yeah. He's perfect—he's good-looking, he's smart, he has a sense of humor, and you're always saying he's kind of a player when it comes to women. And most important, Cam has never met him." I smiled at Nick hopefully. "Think he'll go for it?"

Nick shrugged and reached into his pocket for his cell phone. "I can ask him. Actually, it kind of sounds like the type of crazy plan he'll think is a riot."

"Wait," Allie said before Nick could punch in Charlie's number. "Even if this Charlie guy is willing, how are you going to make sure Cam sees you guys together?"

"That's easy." My mind had already worked out that next step while we were talking. "I'm betting I know what their next date is. Holiday Harmonies is this weekend."

Allie's eyes widened. "Of course! I bet you're right. Everybody goes to that."

The Holiday Harmonies concert was another of the town's myriad annual holiday events. It was a fund-raiser for the Claus Lake Fire Department, traditionally held on the Friday before Christmas. As Allie had said, just about everyone in town attended to socialize with their neighbors, discuss the upcoming Ball, and listen to various local musical groups and soloists do their thing. I figured there was roughly a ninety-nine percent chance that Cam and Jaylene would be there.

"Okay, then." Nick lifted his phone. "Let's see if we can get you a fake date for Friday night."

I looked out the window as Charlie maneuvered his Saab into the last remaining parking space on the block. Dozens of concert-goers were hurrying toward the fireman's hall, most of them with their hands in their pockets and their shoulders hunched against the cold wind gusting in off the lake, which was blowing around the snow that had been falling steadily all day.

"Hang on." I dug into my purse as Charlie cut the engine. "I have the tickets in here somewhere. Let me find them before we get out in the cold."

When I pulled out the tickets, Charlie held out his hand. "Let me hold on to them both until we get inside." He winked. "That's what a *real* date would do, right?"

So far Nick's friend really seemed to be enjoying this whole scheme. Maybe almost *too* much. I couldn't really complain, though. He was just as good-looking as I'd remembered, with mischievous blue eyes, tousled dark hair, and a rakish grin.

"Okay, Prince Charming." I handed over the tickets. "Ready to go in?"

"Can't wait, my love."

Soon we were among the people rushing through the cold and snow. Charlie put one arm around my waist as we walked and reached over and took my hand with his other hand. It felt like overkill, but I didn't complain. It was warmer that way.

"See your ex anywhere yet?" he murmured into my ear as we entered the hall. "Be sure to point him out so I know who my audience is."

I glanced around at the sea of familiar faces. Nick and Allie were just coming back from the coat check window. When they saw me, they hurried over. Nick immediately started into some elaborate high-five ritual with Charlie, but Allie grabbed my arm so tightly it hurt.

"They're here," she hissed. "Over by the snack table."

Looking that way, I saw them. Cam was leaning against the wall, looking casually handsome in cords and the Nordic print sweater I'd bought him for his birthday the previous year. Jaylene was totally overdressed for the occasion in a sparkly midnight-blue dress and high heels, though she didn't appear at all self-conscious about the fact that most of the other female concert-goers wore something closer to my own attire of nice black pants and a sweater. The two of them were chatting with several girls from Jaylene's class.

"Come on," Nick said. "Let's go over and say hi, shall we?"

"Absolutely." Charlie reached over and took my hand. "Shall we, my princess?"

"Sure. Just remember, we're supposed to

be on, like, our second date, okay? Don't go overboard with the princess thing."

"Got it." He winked. "Just having a little fun."

The other girls drifted away as we approached. "Well, hi there, y'all!" Jaylene greeted us with her usual enthusiasm. "Cam said the whole dang town comes to this concert, but Ah guess Ah didn't believe it until Ah got here."

"Yep, we never miss it. We're all addicted to Christmas." Nick gave Cam a friendly slap on the shoulder. "Isn't that right, buddy?"

"Definitely." Cam smiled at him. But I was pretty sure I saw his eyes dart curiously toward Charlie.

Jaylene's curiosity was much more open. "So Lexi," she said with a coy smile. "Who's your handsome friend? Ah don't think we've met." She held out a hand toward Charlie. "Ah'm Jaylene."

"Charlie." He shook her hand. "Nice to meet you, Jaylene. Any friend of the lovely Lexi is a friend of mine."

I tried not to wince. So much for not going overboard. "Charlie, this is, um, my other friend, Cam. Cam, this is Charlie. My—my date."

"Good to meet you, Cam." Charlie held out his hand.

Cam took it. "Likewise."

I tried to watch him without letting on that I was doing it. Was it my imagination, or had his jaw clenched slightly when he'd taken Charlie's hand? I wasn't sure.

"So how did you two meet?" Jaylene asked, snuggling up against Cam until he put his arm around her.

Charlie slung one arm around my shoulders and squeezed. "It's a cute story, actually," he said with a chuckle. "I live over near Dornerville, but I was here in Claus Lake one day last week doing some Christmas shopping. When I stopped at the red light on Elf Street, I looked over and saw the most gorgeous girl I'd ever seen in the car next to me. It was our Lexi, of course." He squeezed again and bent to give me a kiss on the top of my head. "I tried to get her attention, but just then the light changed, and she drove off without even looking over. I was heartbroken."

"Aw, so sweet!" Jaylene cried. "Then what happened?"

Charlie shrugged. "I followed her, of course. What else could I do? I'd been struck by Cupid's arrow." He put his free hand to his chest. "I knew I had to meet her. So I forgot all about my shopping and followed her. I had to run a red light at one point to keep from losing her, and a traffic cop pulled me over. But when I explained, he let me go—he said Lexi Michaels is well known to be the most beautiful girl in town, so he couldn't blame me for chasing her."

If I could have muzzled him at that moment, I would have. Or better yet, strangled him. I'd conveniently forgotten that the main reason Charlie was friends with Nick was because they shared that wicked sense of humor.

"He's just kidding," I said quickly. "He didn't really get stopped by the cops."

Charlie squeezed again. "You don't have to be modest, baby," he said. "Anyone with eyes can see that you're gorgeous. Aren't I right, guys?" He nudged Nick.

Nick coughed. "Uh, she's my cousin, dude."

"Oh, right. Well, I'm sure Cam here agrees with me." Charlie turned and beamed at Cam instead. "Back me up here, buddy."

Cam looked uncomfortable. He shot me a quick glance, then shrugged. "Sure," he said quietly. "Lexi's beautiful."

I felt a pang. How many times had he told me that over the past four years? Somehow, though, I'd never fully appreciated the compliment until right now.

"Sure she is," Jaylene put in happily. "And that's *such* a sweet story, Charlie!"

"Not as sweet as my Lexi." Charlie reached over and chucked me under the chin. "That red light was the luckiest thing that ever happened to me. It was fate, you know?"

I shot Nick a helpless glance. He shrugged at me.

"Um, so did anyone catch the Packers game last weekend?" he spoke up. "Kind of a heartbreaker, wasn't it?"

"The only heartbreaker for me is Lexi," Charlie put in. "It would break my heart if I couldn't be with her."

Things were rapidly spinning out of control. There was no way Cam would believe this guy was for real. Maybe it was better to 'fess up now, admit that Charlie and I were just friends, and play the whole thing off as some kind of joke. . . .

Before I could decide, a buzzer went off to call people into the hall. The concert was about to start.

"Come on, guys," Allie said, sounding relieved. "We'd better go find our seats."

Charlie and I had seats near the middle of the room on the aisle. Nick and Allie were sitting together across the way. Cam and Jaylene were a few rows ahead of them.

"What's the deal with that ridiculous how-we-met story?" I hissed at Charlie as soon as we were sitting down. "Where did you come up with that, some bad romance novel? There's no way anyone would believe that's really how we hooked up."

He leaned back in his seat and grinned at me. "Oh, I don't know. Fact is stranger than fiction, right? Anyway, I think they bought it."

I blew out a sigh. "Well, just cool it a little, okay? Try to keep things more believable."

"Sure, sure. Hey, don't look now, but your pal Cam is looking this way. Let's give him something to look at."

Before I could respond, he leaned over and planted a kiss right in the middle of my forehead. Then he grabbed me and hugged me, running his hands up and down my back.

"Okay, enough." I shoved him back into his own seat before he could get carried away. "This is a family event, you know."

I shot a look toward Cam out of the corner of my eye. He was turned away from me, talking to Jaylene. Had he really looked over and seen me and Charlie just now? Or had that just been another one of Charlie's little jokes?

The house lights started to go down. Just then, I saw Cam turn and look over. His face was somber. When he saw me looking, he immediately turned away again.

My eyes widened even as the place went dark. Was I imagining things, or had he actually looked a little bit . . . jealous?

No way, I thought with a sudden flare of hope as the first singer stepped out onstage. *Could this goofy act of Charlie's actually be working after all?*

I had plenty of time to ponder it over the next hour or so. Finally the last act before intermission came on: a kids' choir. As they began their first song, "I Saw

Mommy Kissing Santa Claus," I had a brainstorm. I leaned closer to Charlie.

"Listen," I whispered, "are you up for a little kissing?"

"Anytime, anywhere, my love," he whispered back, his teeth gleaming in the dark as he grinned at me. "As long as it's you I get to kiss, and not some fat guy in a red suit."

"Good. Let's see if we can get out of here fast at intermission. If we time it right, maybe we can make sure we have an audience for our first kiss, if you know what I mean."

"Reading you loud and clear."

As soon as the lights came up, I dashed across the aisle to where Nick and Allie were sitting. "Get Cam outside," I hissed in Nick's ear.

Then Charlie grabbed me by the hand, and we darted up the aisle and into the lobby. Once there, we immediately headed for the door.

"Wait a second, can't we do this inside?" Charlie complained as I pushed open the door.

"Don't worry, we're not going all the way out." There were two sets of doors leading into the main lobby. In between was a sort of outer lobby, really just a small space with a bulletin board for local announcements and a little table full of safety pamphlets. "I don't want to do this in front of the entire town."

He grinned and stepped closer. "Why not? You ashamed of me?"

"Maybe." There was a window in the door leading inside, and I caught a flurry of movement on the other side. "But never mind that. Kiss me!"

I didn't need to tell him twice. Just as the door swung open, he bent down, wrapped both arms around me, and pulled me to him.

I'd been expecting a first-kiss type of peck on the lips. But what I got was more like a the-world-is-about-to-end-so-kiss-me-dammit type of kiss. I'm talking full contact make-out move. I was so taken by surprise that I just kissed him back. He was actually a pretty good kisser, as far as I could judge—after all, I hadn't really kissed anyone but Cam in a long time.

"Oh, my!" Jaylene's voice broke in with a giggle. "Are we interruptin' something?"

Finally Charlie and I broke apart. I was

feeling a little breathless and discombobulated. Glancing over, I saw Nick, Allie, Cam, and Jaylene standing in the doorway. Nick looked amused. Jaylene looked delighted. And Cam . . . well, I couldn't quite tell how Cam looked. Usually he's as easy to read as a large-print book. But at the moment his face wasn't giving anything away.

"Whoops! You caught us." Charlie grinned with a total lack of shame or sheepishness. "Can you blame me for wanting to sneak off for a little of this?" He reached down and patted me on the butt.

I felt like smacking him. Instead, I forced a smile. "Um, sorry," I said. "Guess we got a little carried away. Come on, Charlie. Let's head back inside."

I didn't quite dare look at Cam again. Was this going to work? Or had I just made a big fool of myself?

Once we were back in the lobby, Jaylene excused herself to go to the ladies' room. Allie went with her. That left me standing there with Nick, Cam, and Charlie.

I shot Nick a pointed look. He caught the hint.

"Hey, Charlie," he said. "I was thinking

of going to grab some drinks at the snack table. Want to come along?"

"No, thanks." Charlie put his arm around me. "I'm not thirsty."

I debated whether stomping on his foot or elbowing him in the ribs would give him the hint more clearly. Before I could decide, Cam cleared his throat.

"Listen, Charlie," he said. "Er, would you mind if I borrowed Lexi for a minute? I—I need to talk to her about something."

My heart leaped into my throat. Well, not really. That would be scientifically impossible. But *something* funny started happening inside of me. Cam wanted to talk to me? That could only mean one thing, couldn't it? My crazy plan must have worked!

"Sure, Charlie doesn't mind," I said quickly, trying to head off any more goofing around. "Right, Charlie?"

Charlie shrugged. "Sure, I guess," he said. "But you have to promise to give her back, okay, buddy?"

"Sure." Cam put a hand on my arm to steer me away from Charlie and Nick. It felt warm and familiar.

We ended up in a quiet corner of the lobby behind the big glass display case full of firefighting suits and stuff. When Cam turned to face me, his expression was still unreadable.

"Sorry to drag you away from your—your date like that, Lexi," he said.

"No, it's okay," I said quickly, my heart beating a little faster. "What is it?"

"I just wanted to tell you something." He shoved his hands in his pants pockets, looking uncertain. "See, ever since we—we broke up, you've been telling me it's for the best. That you loved seeing me with Jaylene, and that sort of thing."

"Yes?" I held my breath.

He shrugged. "Well, even so, I still felt kind of, you know, guilty. And worried about you too—being alone, while I had someone new. You said it was okay, and that you were happy just being friends now, but still . . ." Pulling one hand out of his pocket, he rubbed his head the way he always did when he was trying to figure out how to say something. "Anyway, I know you're good at hiding your emotions sometimes, and I just wasn't sure I'd done the right thing. For both of us. For a while there . . ." He hesitated, then shook his head.

I resisted the urge to reach out, grab him by the collar, and yell *Get on with it!* Instead, I just stood there looking at him in what I hoped was an encouraging manner.

"But never mind all that." Cam smiled uncertainly. "Now I can see that I didn't need to worry. You've moved on. I guess we both have." He shrugged again. "So it seems like this really was meant to be, you know? I have to admit, it was pretty weird to see you kissing another guy like that. But at the same time, it was like a huge weight off my shoulders." He reached over and squeezed me on the arm. "Now I don't have to worry anymore about whether we've done the right thing. I'm glad you and Charlie found each other, Lexi. I hope you'll be really happy with him."

No. My mind refused to take this in. This definitely wasn't what was supposed to happen. . . .

"There y'all are!" Jaylene appeared around the corner of the display case with Charlie right behind her. "Charlie said Ah'd find y'all over here. Come on, they're already shooin' us back in for the second half of the show."

She grabbed Cam's arm. Charlie stepped forward and took mine.

"Yes, we'd better go back in too, darling," he said. "We wouldn't want to miss anything."

I went along with him, my mind completely numb. I didn't even bother to push him away when his arm snaked around my waist again. My eyes and every fiber of my being were fixed on Cam, who was walking with Jaylene just ahead.

I wouldn't have believed it was possible. But it seemed I'd just managed to make things even worse. *Again*.

Fifteen

"Cheer up, Lexi," Allie said with an anxious smile. "You can't just give up."

"Why not?" I glared at her across Nick's dining room table. It was Saturday morning, and the three of us were sitting there wiring together a bunch of fresh evergreen garlands. "In case you've both forgotten, the Ball is less than a week away. The fateful twelfth date."

Nick flicked a juniper berry at me. It bounced off my forehead. "Since when do you have so much faith in her wacked-out theories, anyway?" he demanded. "Usually you're the first one pointing out all the ways they don't make sense. But you're acting like this Dozen Dates thing is, like, the periodic table of elements or something."

I sighed. "I don't need a theory to tell me that things are looking hopeless. All I need are my own two eyes. And my own two ears hearing Cam tell me how thrilled he is that I've finally hooked up with someone so he can fa-la-la-di-da off into the sunset with Jaylene, guilt-free."

Allie and Nick shared a concerned look. "Are you sure you don't want to try talking to him?" Allie suggested tentatively.

"What's the point?" I frowned at the stack of pine fronds in front of me. "I told you, if he finds out everything I've done, he'll totally write me off. I'm sure of it."

"Well, then I have another idea," Allie said. "Want to hear it?"

I shrugged apathetically. "Why not? What do I have to lose? I've already lost Cam, my self-respect, my dignity. . . ."

"This one is called the Heartbreak Charm Theory," Allie said. "I don't think I've told you about it before. But the idea is that guys have a strong protective instinct, and if they think you've been hurt by another guy, that will come out. So for instance, if Cam were to find out that Charlie just dumped you in some totally harsh way, it'll rile up his sympathy and protective impulses. And if you play it right, that could lead to you two getting back together."

"Sounds to me like you should call it the Pity Party Theory." But I couldn't help a glimmer of interest. If any guy would fall for something like that, it was Cam. "Do you really think it could work?"

"Like you said, what do you have to lose?" Nick reached for another evergreen branch. "Want me to see if Charlie's up for a big public breakup scene?"

"No thanks. I've had enough of Charlie's acting skills. Besides, there's not enough time for that." I smiled. "I have a better idea. . . ."

Later that afternoon, Allie sat on my bed next to the cat and watched me put on a pair of gold hoop earrings. I was already dressed in a pair of nice black wool pants, a warm but attractive wool sweater, and the brand-new pair of snazzy high-heeled boots I'd bought earlier that week with the Christmas money my grandfather in Florida had sent.

"You look nice," Allie said.

"Thanks." I smiled at her, a shiver of nervousness passing through me. "Hand me the phone, will you? It's time to call."

Allie tossed me my cell. I caught it and punched in Cam's number. While it rang, I took a deep breath and closed my eyes. I'd already planned out what I was going to say. The only question was, could I pull it off?

"Hello?" Cam's familiar voice answered after a couple of rings, sounding a bit rushed.

"Cam! I'm so glad I caught you." I put a note of panic into my voice.

"Lexi? What is it?" He was instantly on alert, his voice worried. That was Cam for you. "Is something wrong? You sound funny."

I shot Allie a thumbs-up. "I—I'm really sorry to bother you." I did my best to put a little sob into my voice. "But I didn't know who else to call. Allie and Nick aren't answering their phones, and I need to leave for the ceremony soon . . ."

"You mean the tree-lighting ceremony?" he asked.

"Yeah."

The town's annual tree-lighting ceremony

was the keystone of my plan. Like everything else having to do with Christmas in Claus Lake, it was kind of a huge deal. Everyone in town gathered in front of the town hall, the newspaper showed up to take pictures, and the local Girl Scout troop served hot cocoa and cookies and sang carols. Basically, it was the last big public gathering before the Ball.

As that year's Simpson Scholarship winner, I had the honor of placing the big fancy antique star at the top of the tree. Traditionally, the star-placer got all dressed up—well, as dressed up as you could be and still (a) climb a ladder; and (b) not freeze your butt off—and brought along a helper whose job was to hit the switch as soon as the star was in place. That way the newspaper's photographer could get a good shot of the whole shebang while the star-placer was still atop the ladder. A few times in the past, star-placers had brought along a parent, sibling, or best friend to serve as the light person. But since we were talking about high school seniors here, most of them brought a boyfriend or girlfriend as their helper.

In all the commotion over the whole Cam situation, I'd almost forgotten about the ceremony until my conversation with Nick and Allie that morning. On the few occasions it had crossed my mind before then, I'd sort of vaguely assumed that Cam and I would be back together in time for him to go with me.

"Were—were you planning to go to the tree-lighting tonight?" I asked Cam. I threw in a sniffle. Allie nodded approvingly.

"Um, sure," Cam replied. He hesitated. "I'm meeting Jaylene there later. She's going to be a little late, but I was planning to get there in time to see your big moment."

"Oh." I sniffled again. "Look, I normally wouldn't ask, especially at the last minute like this, but like I said, I can't reach Nick or Allie, and my parents already left, and I don't know what to do—" Calling upon my honest feeling of desperation at the thought of losing Cam forever, I dredged up another somewhat dishonest sob. "See, Charlie just—just—just *dumped* me!"

"Oh, Lexi!" He sounded genuinely distressed. "I'm so sorry. You guys seemed so happy last night."

"That's what I thought," I moaned.

"But I was sitting here waiting for him to pick me up for the ceremony, and then he just called, like, five minutes ago and said he decided I wasn't what he was looking for after all."

I felt more than a twinge of guilt at the bald-faced lie. Somehow, it seemed even worse than most of the previous semitruths and vague manipulations. But I tamped down the feeling and plowed on. After all, I was in it this far. What was one more thing to keep from Cam if I ever did win him back?

"So now I don't have a partner for the ceremony, and if I show up alone I'll feel like the world's biggest loser, and so I just thought . . . Is there any way you could flip that switch for me? You know, for old time's sake?"

I held my breath. For a second he didn't answer. I shot a glance at Allie, who was hanging on every word of my end of the conversation. She held up both hands to show me that all her fingers were crossed.

"Um . . . ," Cam said at last. "Wow. I can't believe he did that to you, Lexi. He doesn't even know . . . Well, anyway. I guess—I guess it would be okay. You know, if Jaylene is okay with it, of course."

"Of course." I made my next sniffle especially pathetic. "Do you think she'll let you do it?"

"Let me call her. Like I said, she's going to be late—some relatives are visiting from down South, and they're all having dinner together. So I'm sure she won't mind. I'll call you back in a second, okay?"

"Okay. Thanks."

"Just hang in there, Lexi. It'll be okay." He hung up.

I hung up too, then stared at Allie. "He's calling Jaylene."

Allie looked sort of worried. "Do you think she'll say yes?"

"Why wouldn't she? She's never seemed the least bit threatened by having me around Cam before." I shrugged and set the phone on my desk. "Besides, she's totally clueless about all our weird Claus Lake traditions. She won't have any idea how seriously everybody takes this one, either."

"But Cam does."

"Right. With any luck, I'll be able to use that to my advantage. And by the time poor Jaylene shows up, it'll be too late."

✯

At first everything went perfectly. Cam showed up looking ridiculously handsome in dark pants and a sweater with a shirt and tie underneath, smelling pleasantly of balsam and soap. We walked down the roped-off pathway to the tree area arm in arm while everyone we knew watched and clapped. It felt so much like old times that for a second I wondered if I'd imagined all the rest—my stupid plan, the breakup, Jaylene . . .

We stopped at the base of the tree, an impressive fir draped with hundreds of ornaments and countless ropes of lights just waiting to be set aglow. There was a couple of feet of snow on the ground thanks to the Alberta clipper that had rolled through earlier in the week, but it had been pushed back from around the base of the tree into several large drifts, which only added to the holiday ambience. A podium was set up near the bottom of the tall ladder that stood waiting for me to do my thing. Mrs. Simpson, Principal Jamison, and various other town bigwigs were lined up beside the podium, and Cam and I took our places at the end of the line.

"Congratulations, Miss Michaels," Mrs. Simpson called over to me in her quavery voice. Apparently she'd forgiven me for that scandalous encounter on my front porch. Or maybe she was just senile enough to have forgotten about it. I could only hope. Meanwhile the reporter from the local paper—the same guy who'd documented my earlier shame, by the way—was snapping photos of the whole festive scene. By the way he smirked at me, I could tell *he* hadn't forgotten.

The mayor stepped up to the podium, straightened his candy-cane-print tie, and began his usual speech about the meaning of Christmas in Claus Lake. I didn't really need to listen. Like just about everyone else there, I'd heard it every year of my life. I glanced around quickly, wondering where Nick and Allie were hiding. They'd promised to keep out of sight until after the lighting, just in case Cam had any notions about handing off his duties to one of them.

But at the moment, he appeared content to stand there beside me. "Doing okay?" he murmured as the mayor rambled on, his voice just loud enough for me to hear.

"A little better. Thanks."

"Good. Try not to think about . . . you know." He smiled at me sympathetically. "Hey, remember when Jason Phillips did the honors two years ago?" He chuckled quietly. "He was so terrified of heights that we were all glad there was plenty of snow on the ground in case he fainted and fell off the ladder. I think some of the guys were taking bets on whether he'd make it."

I smiled at him. I could tell he was trying to keep my spirits up, and I loved him for it.

"I remember," I said. "Listen, Cam. Thanks again for doing this. I know it was a lot to ask."

"Not at all." He reached over and gave my hand a squeeze. "That Charlie guy doesn't know what he's missing."

"Thanks." I squeezed back. "Anyway, I'm kind of glad it's you here with me, Cam. It feels right somehow."

"I know what you mean." He didn't take his hand away. "It's weird, but I guess I just always assumed we'd be here together this year for you to do this, you know?"

I nodded. "Me too."

The mayor was winding up his speech

by now. For once, I sort of wished he would ramble on even longer. Cam and I seemed to be making some real progress. Maybe if I could get in a bit more reminiscing time with him before Jaylene showed up . . .

"And so, without further ado," the mayor announced, "I present this year's Simpson Scholarship winner, Miss Alexis Michaels. Come on up here, Lexi!"

I gave Cam's hand one last squeeze. Then I dropped it and hurried over to the base of the ladder. Everyone was clapping, and I gave a self-conscious little wave before grasping the sides of the ladder. It felt weird to have everyone staring at me. But I tried not to think about that as I got ready to climb. As I lifted my boot to the first rung, I glanced over to make sure Cam was in place. He was standing by the switch box. When he saw me looking, he gave me a smile and a thumbs-up. I waved back. Then I turned, accepted the star from the mayor, and started to climb.

It was a little tricky climbing the ladder while also holding the star, which was about the size of my head—hair and all. Only a few rungs up, I realized that the high-heeled boots had probably been a bad idea; they got caught up in the rungs with practically every step. But that hardly seemed worth worrying about. My heart felt lighter than it had in weeks as I thought back over my conversation with Cam.

It really does feel right, us being here together, I thought. *I must have been crazy ever to have thought there were no sparks left between us. He had to be feeling them just now too, right?*

Just then I reached the top. Leaning over carefully, I set the star in place on the clip someone had attached to the tip of the tree. A cheer went up from the crowd below, and the Girl Scouts burst into an enthusiastic if slightly ragged rendition of "O Tannenbaum." Then the lights all over the tree flickered on, bringing more oohs and aahs and cheers from the spectators. I smiled as the newspaper photographer lifted his camera and fiddled with the flash. Cam had done his job.

I glanced down at him. He was still standing by the switch. But this time he wasn't looking at me. He was looking off to the side at . . . Jaylene?

My heart sank like a stone as I saw her appear at the edge of the crowd, leaping giddily through the snow in a pair of ridiculously inappropriate pumps. She flung herself at Cam, grabbed his face in both hands, and planted a big juicy kiss right on his mouth.

No! I couldn't believe it. It wasn't fair. How could she just run in, kiss him like that, and erase everything that had just happened between us?

I guess I must have sort of lunged toward them. I'm not sure why, except that maybe I thought I could peel them apart or something.

But all I really succeeded in doing was losing my balance, being that I was still at the top of the ladder. Oops.

"Whoa!" I cried, forgetting about Cam and everything else for a second as I felt myself sway. My glove slipped off the side of the ladder, and I flailed helplessly in the air for a moment, probably looking like something out of an old Road Runner cartoon. I tried to catch myself with the other hand, but the damp sole of my boot slipped and the heel got caught up in the rung, throwing me further off balance.

Somehow, I managed to hold on with one gloved hand as I slid partway down the ladder. Cries of alarm and surprise were rising from the crowd as people started to notice what was happening. But it was too late for anyone to try to catch me, and I couldn't seem to catch myself. Out of the corner of my eye, I could see the photographer snapping away. Bastard.

I closed my eyes as I felt myself lose my grip on the ladder entirely. My whole body tensed, waiting for the impact. When it came, it was softer than expected but very, very cold. Also, very wet.

If several people hadn't rushed over to pull me out, I would have been happy to lie there in that snowdrift forever. Because just at that moment, it seemed significantly better than the alternative.

Sixteen

My embarrassing tumble off the ladder into the snowbank was pretty much the last straw for me. How many times was I going to insist on publicly humiliating myself before I gave up? What was the point? Cam and Jaylene were as tight as ever. If anything, my behavior seemed to be driving them closer together. Cam was probably relieved to finally have a normal girlfriend instead of being stuck with an exhibitionist nut who had no sense of balance.

"But you can't just give up," Allie insisted as we assembled canapés in my family's kitchen the day after the ceremony.

I shook my head and sighed. "You're such an optimist, Allie. It's sweet. But come on, we need to be practical. The Ball—and that twelfth date—is only three days away." I rested my head on my hand. "Maybe this is fate telling me I was right in the first place. I had good reasons for thinking Cam and I should split up, remember? So why am I second-guessing myself now?"

"Because you and Cam belong together!" Allie looked as if she might cry.

I stuck a caper on a piece of frozen shrimp. "That's what I used to think," I said. "But maybe I was wrong. Maybe we weren't that well-suited after all, and it was just inertia keeping us together all this time."

Over the next couple of days, my mind kept worrying over that. Cam and I were so different. Everyone had always remarked on that. My friends had always insisted that was a good thing—opposites attract, balancing each other out, and all that. But now I wondered. Were we good for each other?

I was pretty sure that Cam had been good for me. He'd helped me relax and not take myself quite so seriously. He'd showed me how to balance out my natural inclination for hard work with a little fun and relaxation. But had any of me rubbed off on him?

In any case, I eventually realized that it didn't matter. Whatever our relationship had been in the past, it was naive to think that it could ever be that way again. Too much had happened over the past few months. I'd reached a sort of critical mass of untruthfulness. Even if I could scheme my way into getting us back together, would I really be able to go on knowing how many lies and secrets I was keeping from him? No, I wasn't sure I'd be able to handle that very well at all. Not with Cam, who was honest and sincere to a fault. It would feel almost like cheating on him. So what was the point, really?

The afternoon before Christmas Eve, I was perched on the edge of the tub in Allie's bathroom. I was supposed to be helping her figure out what shoes and accessories to wear with her angel costume, but my mind kept wandering. When she hurried back to her bedroom at one point for another pair of shoes, I found myself staring at the twin sinks in the room. The one on the right was Allie's. It was mostly tidy but completely random, with not only the usual toiletries occupying its edges but also loose change, several pens and pencils, scrunchies in every imaginable color, and even a paperback book. The other sink was her brother's. It only had a few items sitting on its edges—toothbrush, toothpaste, comb—but it still looked like a mess, encrusted with old smears of Colgate stuck with loose hairs. In my current mood, it seemed like some kind of metaphor. The sinks were paired up, but totally mismatched. Just like me and Cam.

"What about these?" Allie hurried back in wearing a pair of strappy ivory sandals. She stuck out her foot and stared at herself in the full-length mirror that stood between the two sinks. Then she let out a frustrated sigh. "None of these are working at all. I really need some new shoes to go with this costume, but I spent my whole paycheck already." She glanced at me. "I wish we wore the same size. Those white mules you have would be perfect."

"Maybe you could stuff the toes with tissue paper or something," I suggested halfheartedly.

She giggled. "No way! I want to be able

to dance the night away." She twirled in front of the mirror, making the skirt of her costume flare out.

Her chipper mood was wearing on me a little, though I was trying not to let it show. After all, it wasn't Allie's fault that I was feeling so low. No, the blame for that lay squarely on me, myself, and I.

Allie glanced at me in the mirror. Then she turned around to face me.

"Hey," she said. "You're wallowing again, aren't you? Stop that. All we need is the right theory, and maybe you and Cam will be together by the end of the Ball tomorrow. Have we talked about the Hot and Cold Theory yet? Or maybe the—"

"Enough with the theories, okay?" I snapped, finally too fed up to hold in my inner grinch any longer. "All this theorizing doesn't seem to have landed you a date to the Ball, so why should I trust it either?"

I regretted the words as soon as they were out of my mouth. Like I said, Allie could be awfully sensitive about her love life.

In fact, she looked slightly wounded. "Fine," she said. "If you don't want my help, just say so."

"I'm sorry, Allie." I stood up and took a step toward her, a little sick to my stomach. I wasn't sure I could handle it if I messed up another important relationship in my life right now. "I didn't mean that. It was a rotten thing to say. Please forgive me?"

She hesitated, then shrugged and giggled. "Well, okay," she exclaimed, grabbing me and hugging me so tightly that it made her angel wings crinkle. "How can I not forgive you? It's Christmas!"

I hugged her back in relief. All the Claus Lake Christmas cheer was obviously going to her head and making her even giddier and happier than usual. I was glad about that, even if I wasn't feeling it at all this year myself.

"Thanks." I stepped back, and as I smiled at her, I reached a decision. "And listen, I have an idea about your costume. Why don't you scrap the angel thing and wear my Xmas Genie outfit instead? If we roll the hem so the pants aren't too long, it'll look great on you."

Her eyes lit up with interest. But then she frowned. "Wait," she said. "If I wear that, then what will you wear? Your reindeer costume?"

I shook my head. I'd almost forgotten that the outfit Cam and I had picked out way back when was still sitting around in the back of my closet.

"No," I said. "Actually, I think I'm going to skip the Ball this year."

Allie gasped and took a step back. "What?" she exclaimed. "But you can't skip the Ball! Nobody skips it—JoAnn Garson even dragged herself there last year when she had the flu, remember?"

"I know. But I'm really not in a Christmas kind of mood. And I'm even less in a party kind of mood." I stared at her, willing her to understand. "I just think it's better this way."

She stared back. Her dark eyes looked troubled. But finally she nodded.

"Okay," she said quietly. "If that's really your decision, I guess I know better than to try to talk you out of it. It won't be the same without you, though."

"Thanks." I smiled at her, welling up a little as I thought about what a good friend she really was. For a second I almost changed my mind—maybe I could still go, just hang out with Allie the whole time . . . But no. It was better this way. "So how about it?"

I asked her. "Want to wear the genie costume?"

"Oh!" She shrugged, looking a little sheepish. "Well, if you're sure you really won't need it . . ."

"I'm sure."

"All right. I'd hate to see the Triple-Xmas Genie go to waste." She giggled, her joyful mood already seeping back. "I might tone it down to a single X, though. I could ditch the vest and wear my gauzy red beach cover-up over the candy cane thing instead. Oh, and I think I'll wear tights under those see-through pants, too—otherwise my parents will probably disown me." She giggled again. "What do you think?"

"Sounds perfect. You'll have to take lots of pictures, okay?"

Christmas Eve dawned bright, clear, and cold. My parents were in a frenzy of last-minute preparations all day, so I barely saw them. When they finally came home to get changed for the Ball, I told them I had a stomach virus and wouldn't be going. They were surprised but didn't argue. After all the work they'd put in all autumn long, they were totally focused now on going and enjoying the results.

By the time they came downstairs, dressed as a gingerbread cookie (Mom) and a glass of milk (Dad), I was wrapped in my shabby old Polartec robe on the couch watching a rerun of *Rudolph the Red-Nosed Reindeer*. "Looking good, guys," I called to them.

My mom hurried in, pulled off her gingerbread glove, and put her hand to my forehead. "Are you sure you'll be okay here all alone?" she asked.

"Totally," I said. "It was probably just something I ate. I'll be fine."

"Come on, Mellie." Dad toddled in, his legs looking skinny in their white stockings sticking out under the bottom of the milk glass costume. "Lexi's a big girl. She'll be fine. Just call us if you need us, okay, sweetie?"

"Sure, Dad."

The doorbell rang. "That'll be Laurie and Hal," Mom said, hurrying to answer.

Sure enough, Nick's parents were standing on the porch. They were dressed as a lumberjack and a decorated Christmas tree. My uncle was the tree. His ornaments jingled beneath his L.L. Bean parka.

"Lexi! Nick said you weren't feeling well, but I was hoping you'd recover in time to make it to the Ball after all," my aunt said as she entered and spotted me.

"I don't think so," I told her. "I'm going to have to sit this one out."

She tsk-tsk'd a bit. "What a shame. Well, never mind. There's always next year."

There's always next year. I felt a flash of premature nostalgia as I watched my parents and aunt and uncle acting all eager and merry, preparing to go out and have a good time enjoying the fruits of all their labor. No, there wouldn't be a next year for me. Not really. Oh, sure, I'd probably come back to Claus Lake for Christmas and go to the Ball itself. But it wouldn't be the same. The whole extended holiday season was such a part of life in Claus Lake. What would it be like to spend next autumn someplace else—someplace where people probably didn't start humming Christmas carols right after Labor Day? It was a weird thought.

"Oh! I almost forgot." My aunt had been saying something to my mother, but now she turned to my uncle. "Harold, did you remember to bring over the package?"

"What package?" my dad asked as he pulled on his coat. It looked pretty funny trying to stretch over his costume.

My uncle reached into his voluminous jacket pocket and pulled out a brown-paper-wrapped package about the size of a large book. "It's for Lexi. It got delivered to our house a day or two ago by mistake," he said, tracking snow all over the floorboards as he hurried over to me. "In all the commotion, we didn't notice until just now."

That sort of thing was always happening. Even though the same mail carrier had been delivering to our neighborhood for years, our two houses were always getting each other's mail. I suppose that's what came of having two families with the same last name living next door to each other.

"Thanks, Uncle Hal." I took the package without looking at it. "Have a great time tonight, you guys. Have some eggnog for me."

"That's a promise." Dad gave me a wink. "Come on, gang. Let's party!"

They all bustled out, talking and laughing. As soon as they were gone, the house felt a whole lot emptier.

I sighed. Not a creature was stirring.

"Merry Christmas to me," I muttered, feeling sorry for myself.

Not particularly interested in Rudolph's TV antics, I glanced down at the package in my lap. I'd expected it to be a gift from one of my out-of-state relatives. But to my surprise, I saw Cam's name and address on the return label!

I ripped open the package. Beneath the brown shipping paper were a gift-wrapped item and a cream-colored envelope.

My mother had taught me to open the card before the gift. So that was what I did, slitting open the envelope. Inside was a holiday card with a picture of a sprig of holly on the front and Cam's familiar slanty, pointy handwriting inside.

Dear Lexi, it read. *I hope you don't think this is weird. But I came up with the perfect gift for you ages ago, before we broke up, and I still wanted you to have it even if we're not together anymore. I thought it might help inspire you once you get to college. Merry Christmas. Your friend always, Cam.*

Curious now, I grabbed the gift-wrapped package and ripped it open. It was one of those double picture frames. One half held a framed photo and the other a handwritten note. For a second I wasn't sure what it was supposed to be.

Then I gasped as I recognized the sharp-chinned, wild-haired little girl staring out toward the camera. A cheerful, slightly portly man in a white lab coat stood beside her, one hand resting paternally on her shoulder.

"It's me!" I exclaimed aloud to the empty house, grasping the frame in both hands and staring intently at the pair. "And—and is that the doctor from the Mayo clinic?"

My head spun as I tried to understand what I was seeing. It was like gazing directly into the past. Over the years, I'd pretty much forgotten what he looked like. But now it all came back. The horn-rimmed glasses. The good-natured smile. The wisps of graying hair around the edges of his otherwise bald head.

"But how . . . ?" I whispered.

I looked at the note framed beside the photo. The writing was unfamiliar.

Dear Lexi, it said. *I was so touched and honored when your boyfriend contacted me and told me your story. I'm retired now, but naturally I immediately remembered the bright little girl who was so interested in my lab all those years ago. I'm so glad to know that your mother is still doing well, and am especially thrilled to hear that you intend to pursue a science career yourself! I hope you will enjoy this photo—I don't know if you recall, but one of the nurses snapped it that day just by chance. When I retired a few years back, she included it in the scrapbook they all made me. And now I want you to have it. Always stay curious, and please don't hesitate to contact me if you ever need anything. Best wishes, Dr. William J. Ericsson.*

Tears filled my eyes as I read the note a second time. I couldn't believe Cam had done this. How long had it taken him to track down the right doctor? I couldn't imagine how he'd managed it.

My emotions were going crazy as I thought about it. I was so touched by his thoughtful, personal, caring gift that it gave me a sudden surge of new energy—and a new idea. . . .

Seventeen

A few people turned to stare as I walked into the festively decorated fireman's hall a short while later. And no wonder. I was dressed as a reindeer—hind end only. I'd hitched up the extra fabric of the costume with Dad's Christmas suspenders, which were decorated with little wreaths.

The Ball was in full swing. At one end of the hall, a live band dressed as elves was playing a rousing version of "Deck the Halls," and tons of people were dancing and singing along with the "fa la la la la" parts. The walls were draped with the garlands and swags we'd all worked so hard for the past couple of months to make, the ceiling dripped with mistletoe and blinking holiday lights, and the squat blue spruce behind the band was so heavily decorated, there was hardly a needle in sight. The bar and refreshments area was doing a booming business; Mom's shrimp canapés seemed to be a particular hit, since I saw at least three people enjoying them within the first thirty seconds after I arrived. People had been creative with their costumes as usual—in addition to the expected elves, snowmen, and Santas, I spotted an icicle, a potted poinsettia, and a couple of wrapped gifts.

But I took all that in only peripherally, with the detached, perpetually observant part of my mind. Most of my focus was on finding Cam. I looked around for him, but it was hard to see very far in the dense crowd.

I took a few steps farther into the room. "Hi, Lexi," someone said from nearby. "Merry Christmas!"

"Same to you," I replied, glancing over and recognizing my ninth-grade history teacher, who was standing with her husband. They were dressed as what appeared to be a Victorian-era Santa and Mrs. Claus. Or maybe it was Elizabethan era. History was never my best subject. Either way, I gasped as I suddenly caught sight of a couple dancing a few yards beyond them. "Um, would you excuse me?"

I rushed past them and over to the other couple, so shocked by what I was seeing that all thoughts of Cam, the future, and everything else had been wiped out of my mind, at least for the moment. Because that other couple was Allie and Nick. They were dancing together, which was no huge surprise. But they were also *kissing*!

"Hey!" I blurted out, skidding to a stop in front of them. "What's going on?"

Okay, so it wasn't the most tactful approach. But I'd had a rough day. Make that a rough couple of months.

They sprang apart as if I'd hit them with a Taser. "Lexi!" Allie cried, her face immediately going bright red.

Nick kept his composure a little better. "What are you doing here?" he asked. "I thought you were, ahem, 'home sick.'"

"I was. I mean, I— Don't change the subject!" I exclaimed. "I saw you guys— you were totally making out!"

"Would you believe us if we blamed the mistletoe?" Nick asked, squinting upward.

I crossed my arms over my fuzzy reindeer chest. "Try again."

"We're so sorry we didn't tell you, Lexi," Allie cried, grabbing my arm. She looked totally adorable as the Xmas Genie, by the way. The costume suited her much better than me. "We didn't mean to keep secrets. But you were so bummed out about the whole Cam thing, and then once a few weeks had gone by, it just seemed kind of awkward. . . ."

"Wait, *what?*" I was really having trouble taking this in now. My scientific mind had already started plugging the strange little scene I'd just interrupted into a logical sequence. They'd come to the Ball, neither with another date; they'd danced together, gotten a little carried away . . . But no. It sounded like there was a lot more to it than that.

Nick took a deep breath. "Okay, here's the deal," he said. "Allie was really cool to me after Rachel and I broke up. Especially since, um, a lot of people were, you know, kind of distracted by other things."

I felt a pang of guilt. Come to think of it, I hadn't really paid that much attention to Nick's heartbreak after the first week or two. Not only had I been distracted by the whole Cam situation, but also by the

SATs, the Simpson Scholarship, my classes at school . . .

"Anyway, we started getting kind of, you know, close," Allie picked up the story. "Then a while ago, the two of us spent a lot of time together working on the kids' room decorations, remember? That's when we realized we were starting to like each other as, um, more than friends."

"Oh." I blinked. "Wait. So like, that time I stopped by your house when you guys were making the paper chains . . ."

I paused as Allie giggled and shot Nick a glance. He grinned.

"Yeah, that was interesting timing," he told me. "If you'd barged in about thirty seconds earlier, you would've interrupted our first kiss."

"Really?" I thought back, trying to remember the details of that day. I'd been pretty wrapped up in my own stuff at the time, what with having just survived that disastrous dinner with Andrew and realizing how colossally wrong I'd been to let Cam go. Even so, how had I missed the clues? If I'd been paying more attention, would I have caught them sooner?

Allie was peering at me with concern.

"Are you mad at us for not telling you?" she asked. "We wanted to. But we weren't sure you were ready to deal with it. You know, considering your state of mind with the Cam thing and all."

"Yeah," Nick said. "We figured it would be better to wait until you and Cam were back together." He shrugged. "Who knew it would take so long?"

I wasn't sure what to say. My cousin and my best friend, a couple . . . I was awed and confused and surprised and a little weirded out by this unexpected romance that had happened right under my nose without my ever noticing. So much for my observant scientific nature. Not to mention my worries about not wanting anything in our tight little group to ever change.

"Oh," I said. "Um. Well, I can't say I'm not surprised. But I'm pretty sure that once my brain is working again, I'll think this is a good thing." I smiled. "Congratulations. I'm happy for you two. And I might forgive you for keeping this secret if you promise to tell me everything now. Or, rather, a little later. Right now I have something I came here to do."

"Really?" Allie shot a look at Nick. He

raised his eyebrows curiously. But neither of them asked any questions. That was a couple of really good friends for you.

I gave them a wave and moved off through the crowd. My shock at what I'd just found out was fading a little, and my mind was getting back to the reason I was here.

It only took another minute or two to locate Cam and Jaylene. They were standing at the edge of the dance floor, watching the action out there and nibbling at a shared plate of snacks. Cam was dressed as a very handsome Nutcracker. Jaylene looked even more incredible in her Naughty Elf costume than she had at the store. Seeing them standing there together, totally wrapped up in each other, I almost lost my nerve. But I shoved that aside, took a deep breath, and walked right up to them.

"Hi, Lexi! Merry Christmas." Jaylene scanned my half-reindeer getup, looking a little confused. "Uh, cute outfit."

"Thanks. Yours too," I replied. "Um, can I borrow Cam for a sec? It's important."

"No problem, Lexi." Jaylene seemed as unperturbed by my presence as usual. "Ah was just going to visit the little girls' room anyhow."

She wandered off. I grabbed Cam by the arm and dragged him away, barely allowing him enough time to set his plate down on a table nearby.

"What is it, Lexi?" he asked. "And what happened to the other half of the costume? If you thought I still had it, I brought it over to your house weeks ago, remember? Although it's really made for *two* people, so I don't know if—"

"No, it's not that." I turned to face him. We had just left the main hall and were now in a quiet hallway that led back to some dark and empty offices. "I only wore the bottom half of the costume on purpose. That's because I realized I've been a real ass lately."

"Huh?" He looked startled.

"It all started a few months ago at that big last-day-of-freedom party at the lake the night before our first day of senior year . . . ," I began.

And then I proceeded to tell him the truth. About deciding we would be better off splitting up. About setting him up with Jaylene. About all the crazy things I'd done since then trying to win him back.

"So basically, I've been a total moron,"

I finished. "But it's all because I didn't really appreciate what I had with you until it was gone."

He hadn't said a word all through my confession. By the end he looked as stunned as someone who'd just been run over by Santa's sleigh, including all eight reindeer.

"Wow," he said at last, his tone and expression completely blank. "I can't believe it."

My heart sank. Had I just blown it? Judging by the look on his face, I was afraid my earlier fears had been right. Now that he knew everything, it could very well be the end of any chances we might have had.

Eighteen

But then: a Christmas miracle. Cam smiled.

"Wow," he said again. "I know how hard that must have been for you."

"Huh?" I said. "You mean being apart from you?"

He chuckled. "No," he said. "Well, okay, maybe that too. But I was talking about how tough that must have been just now—you coming out like that and admitting your mistakes. And your fears about the future. And your lack of control."

Okay. So maybe he did know me pretty well.

"Um, yeah. Kind of. Maybe," I admitted, realizing it was true. All this time I'd been using his own honesty as an excuse not to tell him the truth. And that really had been part of it. But maybe another part had been not wanting to admit I was wrong. I'd been a straight-A student for a long time. I wasn't used to making many big mistakes.

He gazed at me, still smiling. "A lot of people probably don't realize how cautious you can be about some things, Lexi," he said. "You're so direct, it's easy to assume you never have any doubts or fears about anything. But I've seen the way you can sort of hide behind that directness, you know?"

I didn't, actually. At least not until he said it. But again, I realized he was right. Maybe sometimes I did just plow ahead when I might be better off admitting I didn't know what the heck I was doing. I would have to think more about that later.

"I didn't want you to know what I'd done," I told him, not ready to let myself off the hook just yet. "I figured you'd be shocked and horrified by how I'd been so manipulative and dishonest and stuff."

"Horrified, maybe." He winked. "But actually, now that I'm clued in, I can't say

I'm really all *that* surprised. Science geek or not, nobody can say you're not creative!"

I laughed a little, finally starting to relax as I realized he really wasn't going to hold this against me. But then my nervousness returned as I realized we were still dancing around the main point.

"So," I said, calling up that directness he'd just been talking about. "I guess I'm asking you to make a choice here, huh?" I swallowed hard, trying not to picture Miss Sexy Elf waiting for him back in the other room. "Me or Jaylene."

He glanced down at the floor for a moment. Lifting one hand, he ran it over his face and up through his hair, dislodging the little soldier's cap from his Nutcracker costume. I felt queasy. This was it—after he answered, I would know my fate for sure. If he chose Jaylene, I only hoped he'd let me down easy. . . .

Then he looked up again and met my eye. "Don't be an idiot," he said, his voice suddenly hoarse and low. "That's no choice at all, Lexi. It's you. It's always been you and only you for me."

I gasped, relief flooding through me

so violently that my knees wobbled and I was afraid I might have to sit down. "Really?"

"Of course. These past few weeks have driven that home more than ever." He blew out a loud sigh. "It was killing me to think things might really be over between us. The only reason I went along with the whole Jaylene thing in the first place is because she was so totally different from you in every way. I thought maybe that would distract me a little once I got to be pretty sure you were pulling away." He smiled rather wanly. "See? I can pick up a hint. And I knew if you'd decided you didn't want to be with me anymore, there was no point trying to change your mind."

"That sounds just like what Nick and Allie keep telling me," I murmured. "Am I really that stubborn?"

"Let's just call it determined. Anyway, I figured it was better to let you go with some dignity if you'd made up your mind. That way I figured at least maybe we could still be friends."

"Yeah. I always definitely wanted us to

stay friends too. I couldn't imagine not having you in my life." I gazed at him thoughtfully. "But listen, Cam, if you really thought I was making a mistake or treating you unfairly or whatever, you should have said something. It may seem like I want to make all the decisions all the time, but I don't. Especially not if it means you might be unhappy."

He bit his lip. "I hear you. Guess maybe I need to stand up for myself a little more from now on?"

"Yeah." I smiled at him. Okay, so maybe we both had a few things to work on. But it was worth it if it meant being together.

That reminded me . . .

"Oh," I said. "Um, so who's going to break it to Jaylene?"

"I don't know." Cam sounded dubious. "I mean, she has those long fingernails, and I'm pretty sure her dad owns a shotgun. . . ." Seeing the startled look on my face, he laughed. "Kidding! I'll take care of it. As long as *you* promise never to put us through anything like this again."

I quickly crossed my heart with one finger. "That's a promise I'm happy to make." My heart leaped with something—tidings of comfort and joy, maybe?—and I was itching to grab him and kiss him just to make it all official. But I had a feeling he wouldn't be comfortable with that quite yet. Not until he'd settled things with Jaylene. He was that kind of guy, after all.

"Be right back," he promised.

"I'll be waiting."

He hurried off. As soon as he was gone, I dug into the waistband of my reindeer butt and fished my cell phone out of the pocket of the pants I was wearing underneath. I was bursting with my good news and couldn't wait to share it, but I also wasn't ready to go out there and risk running into Jaylene at the moment. So I quickly sent a text message to Allie's phone.

She texted back within seconds. Her message was so full of exclamation points that I could hardly decipher it. I guessed that meant she was happy for me.

It was only a few minutes before Cam returned. "Well?" I demanded.

"She took it pretty well, actually. Guess that means I wasn't the man of her dreams after all." He smiled wryly. "In fact, she's already comforting herself by dirty dancing with Bruce."

Easy come, easy go. That seemed to be how Jaylene viewed her love life. Then again, maybe there was something to Allie's Dozen Dates Theory after all. . . .

Cam saw me smiling. "What?" he asked.

"Nothing," I said. "I'll tell you later. Right now, I'm still trying to figure out why it took me so long to just be honest with you. Maybe—maybe it's because I wasn't being honest with myself when I decided I needed to break up with you."

"What do you mean?"

"I mean I might be a little more nervous than I wanted to admit about that fabulous future I have planned for myself." I shot him a sheepish glance. "I know I always talk about how I'm looking forward to going away to some great school, living in a big city . . . but it's going to be a huge change, you know?"

He nodded. "I know. But you're going to be great. I'm sure of it."

"Thanks. But if I'm out there and you're still here—"

"It won't matter," he put in. "Lexi, nobody can predict the future. We'll just have to take it as it comes. But I can promise you one thing—I would never make you choose between going after your goals and being with me." He shrugged. "I know I talk about that little restaurant on Elf Street. But you have to understand, my heart isn't set on that the way yours is on your career stuff." He reached for my hand and smiled that open, honest, easy smile of his. The smile of a kid on Christmas. "Nope, the only thing my heart is set on is being with you. Whatever it takes, we'll work it out."

Stepping forward, I wrapped my arms around him. I felt his encircle me in their familiar way, strong and gentle at the same time. He bent his head toward me, and as soon as we kissed, I knew he was right. Whatever it took, we could do it. Together. It was Christmas Eve in Claus Lake, all was right with the world, and the future could wait.

When we finally came up for air, Cam smiled down at me. "Hey," he said, "I almost forgot. Did you get my present? What did you think of it?"

"I loved it," I answered truthfully.

But as he bent to kiss me again, I couldn't

help thinking happily that all I'd ever *really* wanted for Christmas was him. It was a good thing that I'd finally figured that out—just in the Old Saint Nick of time.

About the Author

Catherine Hapka has never dressed up as a Christmas Genie, but she always enjoys the holiday season nonetheless. She has written more than one hundred and fifty books for children and young adults. In addition to reading and writing, she enjoys horseback riding, animals of all kinds, gardening, music, and traveling. She lives on a small farm in Chester County, Pennsylvania, with a couple of horses, three goats, a small flock of chickens, and too many cats.

LOL at this sneak peek of

Sea of Love

By Jamie Ponti

A new Romantic Comedy from Simon Pulse

Love at first sight is supposed to happen when locking eyes on a busy Parisian street corner or while sharing a booth during a poetry reading at a crowded SoHo coffee shop. It's not supposed to take place while you're on a rooftop in the middle of night spying on a guy like some pathetic perv. Unfortunately, I seem totally incapable of doing anything the way it's supposed to be.

It wasn't technically *first* sight. I had seen Zach countless times before, just never with the roller-coaster drop in my stomach or the sudden shift of cabin pressure in my head. As for the spying, there was no premeditation or intent to stare. (At worst it makes me a second-degree Peeping Tom.)

It happened on New Year's Eve, as the worst year of my life was mercifully coming to a very dull and uneventful end. All of the New Year's essentials like cool music, good friends, and a boyfriend to kiss at midnight were glaringly absent.

It was just me—all alone—on the roof of a decrepit hotel overlooking godforsaken Coconut Beach, Florida. (Okay, "decrepit" and "godforsaken" are a bit harsh, but since this happened a few minutes before my resolution to be less negative and dramatic, I think they're acceptable and appropriate.)

The moment was in stark contrast to the previous New Year's, which I spent at Hadley Montgomery's townhouse on the Upper East Side. Had's family is sick rich, and the party was loaded like a Lexus. They had a rocking band and shrimp the size of my head. At midnight, when I kissed my boyfriend, Brendan, I closed my eyes, knowing that my life was perfect. Fast-forward three hundred sixty-five days and my eyes are wide open to a very imperfect world.

It would have been one thing if we had come to Florida on some sort of lame family vacation. At least then it would have been tolerable. I could have acted like I was having a good time while secretly counting the seconds until a flight would carry us back to civilization.

But there would be no flight to catch and no civilization to call home. We were not just staying at the hotel. We had moved in—permanently!

I'll skip the rancid details. Just know that my father had a full-on midlife crisis and somehow convinced my mom to go along for the ride. (Here's the part I didn't get. If it was *his* crisis, why was I the one who had to suffer?) He quit his job on Wall Street, cashed out all of his investments, and sold our sweet TriBeCa apartment two blocks from the building where Gisele Bündchen lives. (Not that the two of us hung out or anything, but it was more than a little nice to think we went to the same Starbucks.)

Then he put all of the money together and bought the Seabreeze Hotel. If that sounds glam, believe me, it isn't. The Seabreeze isn't one of those cool hotels in South Beach with Crayola colors and a lobby full of people who look like they're ready for a fashion shoot. It's strictly an old-school wooden dinosaur with guests who are a lot more *America's Funniest Home Videos* than *America's Next Top Model*.

The hotel has two main floors, which

stretch along the beach so that each room has an ocean view. The third floor is much smaller and only has five rooms, which connect to form a suite. That's where we live. Officially, it's called the penthouse. (As if.) There's even a PH button instead of a 3 in the elevator. (I like to say the PH stands for "piehole.")

Our place looks kind of like the top tier of a wedding cake. I can step over the railing of my balcony directly onto the roof. I keep an old aluminum beach chair hidden up there, and whenever I want to get away from everything, I can slip out onto the roof and practically disappear. Lately this had been an extremely frequent urge. That's why I was up there on New Year's Eve.

There was a pretty decent-sized party going on downstairs in the hotel ballroom. It was a fifty-fifty mix of hotel guests and locals, with a band that played covers of pop songs. I hung tough until they decided to bust out "YMCA." That's when I bolted.

I knew it was lame of me not to stay. (Maybe even lamer than their version of "YMCA.") After all, my mother and little brother had completely turned around, so I was the only one still protesting the move. But I was in no mood to party. I faked an upset stomach to get out of it. There was no way my mom believed me, but she let me come upstairs anyway. I think she'd just gotten tired of trying to convert me.

As I sat back in my chair and looked out at the ocean, I could hear the people two stories below counting down the final seconds of the year. They got louder with each one until the clock struck midnight, and then they all blew on toy horns and yelled, "Happy New Year!"

That's when the guilt kicked in. I considered feigning a miraculous recovery and going back down to the party as part of a whole turning-over-a-new-leaf-in-the-new-year kind of thing. But something on the beach caught my eye.

It looked like a person carrying a large object into the water. I've probably seen way too many episodes of *CSI: Miami*, because my first instinct was that it was someone trying to dump a dead body into the ocean. In truth I couldn't tell what it was. There was a half moon, but it was also really cloudy out, which made it hard to see.

As the clouds drifted across the sky, little bursts of light broke through and let me take a better look. I realized that the person wasn't carrying a body; he was carrying a surfboard. Just like that this guy went from being interestingly criminal to positively idiotic. Only a moron would surf in the middle of the night.

Even without the dead body, I thought about calling the police. It's not against the law to go surfing at night. (Actually, I don't know that. It may very well be.) But I was worried the guy might have had a few too many New Year's cocktails. If he went out into the water drunk, he could easily drown.

But this guy didn't move like he was drunk. In fact he didn't even move like it was nighttime. He glided across the sand and picked up speed as he sprinted through the shallow water, lifting his legs up just high enough to clear the surface. Finally, he slid onto the board and began to paddle out.

I shivered just thinking about how freezing the water must have felt. He was wearing a wet suit, but it only covered his arms down to the biceps and his legs down to the thighs. He didn't seem to mind, though. He never made a noise or acted like it was the slightest bit cold. He just paddled silently out to the swells. When he got there, he sat up on the board with his legs dangling over the sides. He glanced back at the beach just as a cloud shifted, and I was able to get a look at his face. Even though he was out pretty far, I knew it was Zach.

That's why it wasn't first sight. I had seen Zach plenty of times before. He works part-time bussing tables in the hotel dining room. He's pretty cute and extremely quiet. And, as this escapade hints, he's more than a little weird.

As part of the family, I pitch in to help at the hotel. I wait tables in the dining room three nights a week. In the three months we'd worked together before New Year's Eve, I don't think Zach and I had spoken for more than a total of ten minutes.

I couldn't figure out what he was doing out there, but for some reason I couldn't stop watching. He was just a dark shadow bobbing up and down on the swells, looking for a wave to catch, and I was mesmerized.

The entire episode seemed insane. Not only was the water freezing, but I assumed that nighttime would be when all of the sharks and other deadly sea creatures come out. Whether that was true or not, Zach obviously wasn't worried. Even from as far away as the hotel roof, I could see that he was smiling and totally enjoying himself. Finally, after a few minutes, a set of three waves started to come at him. He lay out flat on the board and started to paddle back in the same direction as the waves. He floated up and over the first two before finally latching onto the last one.

I have to admit it looked pretty freaking cool in the moonlight as he climbed up onto the board, the top of the wave forming a silvery wash at his feet. Even though it wasn't a particularly big wave, he was able to stay up almost all the way in before finally stepping off into the shallow water.

That was it. He only rode that one wave. When it was over, he got up out of the water and carried his board back onto the beach. A breeze kicked up, strong enough to make the palm trees sway, and for the first time he looked cold.

He unzipped his wet suit and stripped

down to a pair of board shorts, shivering as he toweled off. (Here's a fact I had never noticed in his busboy outfit: Zach is kind of ripped.) Once he was all dry, he threw on a T-shirt and carried his board back up toward the hotel parking lot.

This is where the perv gene kicked in. I couldn't stop staring at him. It was one thing when he was on the ocean; I could argue that I was staring at him for safety reasons. But here the only explanation was unbridled hormonal intrigue.

As he reached the streetlight at the edge of the parking lot, he looked right up at me. It was as if he'd known I was there all along. Purely by instinct I pressed myself back into the shadows to hide. I don't know why. It wasn't like I was doing anything wrong—maybe a little weird, but not wrong. For a moment we just held the look. Then he flashed a smile of epic proportions. Perfect white teeth, dazzling even in the darkness. They were impossible to ignore. I smiled back and gave him my best nonchalant wave. Like it was totally normal for me to be on the roof of the hotel and for him to be surfing at midnight on New Year's Eve.

Then he walked out of the light and disappeared into the darkness. It was in that instant that I had the roller-coaster/cabin-pressure effect. I plopped down in my little beach chair for a second and tried to figure out what it all meant. But I didn't have much time to think about it, because I heard the elevator kick into gear. The rear elevator only goes to the third floor, so I knew it had to be my parents or my brother heading up to the piehole. Luckily, like everything else in the hotel the elevator is ancient and slow. I had more than enough time to fold up my chair and climb in through my window.

I jumped right into bed and did my best to look like I was suffering from a raging upset stomach. My mother knew that I wasn't really sick. And she knew that I knew that she knew. But you still have to go through the motions and play out the entire scene. That's just what mothers and daughters do.

After a few moments there was a knock on the door, and I was ready for my performance. I expected my mother to come in and make sure I wasn't goofing off, and I was going to greet her with deep bronchial hacking. But it wasn't Mom. It was my dad.

"How are you feeling, Darby?" Unlike Mom, Dad probably thought I really was sick.

"Better," I said with a faint cough, now feeling very guilty.

"Well, I just wanted to stop by and wish you a happy new year."

"Happy New Year, Dad."

He looked at me for a long moment and then said something totally unexpected. "I did a terrible thing to you, Darby, and I'm sorry. Making you move right before your senior year is unforgivable."

I wanted to scream, *That's right! It's totally, horribly, irrevocably unforgivable!* But a New Year's resolution should last at least more than eleven minutes. Besides, with regard to everything else in my life, my dad has always been great. I looked back into his eyes, which seemed filled with concern.

"It's not unforgivable," I said, trying to make myself believe what I was saying. "I don't understand it, but I can forgive it. In fact, I already have."

He flashed me a big smile, leaned over,

and kissed me on the forehead. He lingered for a moment with his cheek against my forehead. That's the way he used to check my temperature when I was little and had a fever. I couldn't tell if he was doing it to see if I was sick, or just to go back to a time before I had become such a drama queen.

When he stood up, I saw that my mom had come into the room behind him. She was obviously pleased with what she had seen and heard. As a result she didn't give me a hard time about the pseudo stomach ailment. She just looked at me and smiled.

"Happy New Year, Darby."

"Happy New Year, Mom."

It was the closest thing we'd had to a tender moment since we came to Florida.

After they left, I just lay there in my bed and tried to make sense of the year that was and get my head around the year that was coming. It may have been starting out in Coconut Beach, but it would end with me going off to college. (By the way, the anxiety of waiting for admissions letters also wasn't doing much to help my general mood.)

I followed my normal nighttime routine and looked at my computer screen as I fell asleep. My screen saver was set to be a slide show from back home in New York, with more than fifty pictures in the loop. There were pictures of me and my best friends during all sorts of capers. There were images of some of my favorite New York landmarks, like the Chrysler Building, Central Park, and the Brooklyn Bridge. And there were a lot of pictures of me and my old boyfriend, Brendan.

The thing that was weird was that Brendan and I had never really broken up. My family moved to Florida, and that was the end of the relationship. There'd been no mention of long-distance romance, so we weren't still a couple. But there'd also never been a final moment. That's why I still had his pictures on my computer.

But when I finally closed my eyes to fall asleep, the last image in my mind was not New York or Brendan. It was Zach looking up at me and flashing that smile. As smiles go, I would classify his as dazzling. It also had a hint of mystery. I didn't know if he was smiling with me or smiling at me. Was he laughing at the fact that he'd caught me looking at him? Or was he saying something else?

What's life without a little . . .

DRAMA!

★ A new series by Paul Ruditis ★

At Bryan Stark's posh private high school in Malibu, the teens are entitled, the boys are cute, and the school musicals are *extremely* elaborate. Bryan watches—and comments—as the action and intrigue unfold around him. Thrilling mysteries, comic relief, and epic sagas of friendship and love . . . It's all here. And it's showtime.

From Simon Pulse • Published by Simon & Schuster

Funny. Fresh. Fabulous.

Don't miss these books by Julie Linker:

From Simon Pulse

Published by Simon & Schuster

"Once upon a Time"

is timely once again as renowned heroines master newfound destinies, uncovering a unique and original **"happily ever after. . . ."**

Belle
Cameron Dokey

The Night Dance
Suzanne Weyn

The Crimson Thread
Suzanne Weyn

Sunlight and Shadow
Cameron Dokey

The Rose Bride
Nancy Holder

Golden
Cameron Dokey

Before Midnight
Cameron Dokey

The Storyteller's Daughter
Cameron Dokey

From Simon Pulse
Published by Simon & Schuster

PULSE it

Did you **love** this book?

Want to get the hottest books **free**?

Log on to
www.SimonSaysTEEN.com
to find out how you can get
free books from **Simon Pulse**
and become part of our **IT Board**,
where you can tell **US**, what **you** think!

SIMON PULSE